Tarian Silver Lion

(New Tarian Pride, Book 2)

Grim Christmas

(Daughters of Beasts, Book 4)

New Vyr

(Daughters of Beasts, Book 5)

T. S. JOYCE

Tarian Silver Lion
Grim Christmas
New Vyr

ISBN: 9781797409986
Copyright © 2019, T. S. Joyce
First electronic publication: February 2019

T. S. Joyce
www. tsjoyce.com

NOTE FROM THE AUTHOR:

This book is a work of fiction. The names, characters, places, and incidents are products of the writer's imagination or have been used fictitiously and are not to be construed as real. Any resemblance to persons, living or dead, actual events, locale or organizations is entirely coincidental. The author does not have any control over and does not assume any responsibility for third-party websites or their content.

Published in the United States of America

First digital publication: November 2018
First print publication: November 2018

Editing: Corinne DeMaagd
Cover Photography: Wander Aguiar, Andrey Bahia
Cover Model: Wander Aguiar, Jonny James, Tyler Halligan

DEDICATION

For book worms.
You make the world go round.

ACKNOWLEDGMENTS

I couldn't write these books without some amazing people behind me. A huge thanks to Corinne DeMaagd, for helping me to polish my books, and for being an amazing and supportive friend. Looking back on our journey here, it makes me smile so big. You are an incredible teammate, C!

Thanks to Wander Aguiar, Jonny James and Tyler Halligan, the cover models for these short stories. And thank you to Wander Aguiar and Andrey Bahia, and their amazing team for these shots for the covers. You always get the perfect images for what I'm needing.

And last but never least, thank you, awesome reader. You have done more for me and my stories than I can even explain on this teeny page. You found my books, and ran with them, and every share, review, and comment makes release days so incredibly special to me.

1010 is magic and so are you.

Grim Christmas

(Daughters of Beasts, Book 4)

ONE

The Reaper was being hunted.

A twig snapped behind Grim, and he yanked the ax to a halt mid-swing. With narrowed eyes, he glared over his shoulder at the snowy woods, but just like every other time he'd stopped his work to punish whoever was fucking with him, the woods were quiet and still.

Too quiet.

Too still.

"Rhett, if this is you playing some stupid game instead of working, I'm going to murder you."

No answer.

The tree Grim was hacking at with the ax would hold, so he turned all the way around and lifted his chin, scented the air. He gripped the wooden handle until it creaked in complaint. He couldn't smell anything but snow and pine. His mate, Ash, was in town interviewing for a job, Juno was in town with her, Remi was working on winterizing the beer shed, Kamp was on the next mountain over loading logs, so the closest one to Grim would be the jokester slash country singer of the crew, Rhett.

When a pair of ravens suddenly flew up from a tree, Grim tensed and watched their escape into the sky.

There was something red on the ground ahead. It looked so bright against the snow. God, he wished Ash was here. He'd been on edge for days and couldn't figure out why. The whole Crew swore he was being crazier than normal, but he was actually trying to be the Alpha they deserved. That was impossible to do if Rhett kept messing with him.

Grim crunched through the snow and came to a stop right in front of a red Santa hat lying crumpled on the ground.

He hated the holidays. Hated them with a passion ever since his second lion, the Reaper, had come to be. Holidays had never been the same after he lost his mind.

And now Rhett, that twathole, was shoving it in his face.

Punish him.

Grim stooped and picked up the hat and, choking both that and the ax, strode east for Rhett's jobsite. The Reaper didn't like being teased, didn't like being taunted, and there was no stopping the anger roiling in his blood now. Rhett should've been working instead of playing pranks on Grim. If Ash were here, she would be the only one who could stop him from what he was about to do.

But she wasn't, and so the Reaper was free to be the Reaper—the rip-roaring, vengeful, dark-souled monster everyone knew him to be.

Rhett's games ended now.

TWO

Ash bit back the burning tears that threatened to paint her cheeks with weakness. She yanked off her fanciest boot, the right one, the one without scuffs all over the toe from where she'd fallen on the curb at her last interview for Barney's Furniture Mart. The nicest boot she owned. She ripped that little knee-high smexy shoe right off her foot. Or she tried to, but the dang zipper was still done up on the inside of her calf, securing her in an ankle-cage like it had been Super-Glued to her leg. With a little high-pitched screech, she unzipped it—twice on account of the zipper getting stuck on her skinny jeans—and then she finally, finally, anti-climactically, yanked it off. Now she super wanted to cry.

After setting the pair of "interview boots," as she called them, to the side in a pile of freezing snow, she pulled on her fur-lined snow boots one by one. She wouldn't slip on ice in these. They had tread as thick as tires.

Gah, that was the worst interview she'd ever been on. Embarrassment heated her cheeks, and she shrugged into her jacket to ward off the frigid breeze. She needed some magic, so she reached into her pocket and pulled out a half piece of gum, a tuft of lint, and a penny she'd found heads-up on the snow as she'd walked into the library for this interview. The fountain where she sat on the edge was turned off for the winter, but that didn't stop her from tossing the penny over her shoulder and making a wish as the dang copper coin bounced off the frozen water behind her.

I wish I could get a job before Christmas.

It wouldn't be as potent as a 10:10 wish, but it was 11:13 a.m. right now, a loooong day ahead of her to make that wish tonight.

She wasn't going to be able to get her mate, Grim, what she really wanted to buy him for Christmas. Sure, she had a credit card, but she didn't feel comfortable charging to it when she had no way to make the payments at the end of the month.

Ash huffed a frozen breath and frowned at the bustling street in front of the library. Everyone was in town doing their last-minute Christmas shopping. Usually, she liked people-watching, making up nice stories about the passersby, but today, she just wanted to climb in the passenger's seat of Juno's car and wallow in her disappointment.

Gads, it was colder than a beer on ice out here. Her nipples were like little marbles. Grim would approve.

Ash's lip pouted out, and she didn't even try to tuck it back in. She'd done everything right. She'd made sure she was qualified to work in the library, she'd sent in her resume, got two references, dressed nice, and had even dyed her blue hair red to coordinate with Christmas. Yeah, it was still not as subtle as her natural black hair, but it was quieter than bright blue.

Where in hades was Juno?

Blowing out a toot noise with her lips, she pulled her phone out and typed, *Interview is done, can you pick…* But before she finished the text, an engine revved down the street, and here came one of her besties, blaring a hip-hop version of "Jingle Bells" out the open windows of her car.

Ash watched with her eyes so wide, the cold air threatened to freeze them open. Juno slammed on the brakes and drifted to a stop in front of the library. What the hell had gotten into her?

"Ash!" Juno said, hanging out the driver-side window. "Ash!"

Ash looked around. "Why are you yelling? You can see I'm looking right at you, right?"

"We got mail!" Juno crowed, holding up a fistful of envelopes. "Lots and lots of mail!"

Maybe her friend had been drinking. Ash should probably drive.

Ash stood while gathering up her purse and fancy but pointless interview boots and shuffled across the icy sidewalk to Juno's car. But when she tried to dump her curvy butt unceremoniously into the passenger's seat, she couldn't because it was already taken up with about fifty colorful envelopes that were dripping off the seat and onto the floorboard.

"What is this?" she asked, picking one up to study the address.

Rogue Pride Crew

1010 Wayward Way, Tillamook, Oregon

The return address simply said *Almost Alpha, Gray Backs, Damon's Mountains*

When she looked back at Juno, who was sitting on the open windowsill and hanging onto the roof of her car, she was grinning at Ash like her face was frozen.

"Is your mouth okay?" Ash asked, concerned.

"It's Christmas cards from the Crews."

Ash gasped and ripped one open.

Have an ornamental holiday season.

From Willa. And Matt. But mostly Willa because Matt didn't want to take this picture but I made him so technically it's from both of us. Drink lots of eggnog.

Willamena Barns

The picture was of Willa and Matt hanging upside down from a tree by ropes at their ankles. They were dressed in festive, sparkly-silver onesies. Like living ornaments. Willa was grinning from ear to ear but Matt, who was beside her, had his arms crossed and a grumpy look on his face. His branch bent so far down his head almost touched the ground.

Ash cracked up and handed it to Juno.

"Oh, my gosh, Juno! We're in the Christmas card

loop now!" Ash said on a breath.

"Yeah," Juno whispered. "We finally have a Crew to join in. You know what that means, don't you?"

"Safety, eating together, and trying to get along—"

"No, no, no, not what a Crew means. I mean, now we have to join in on the fun, right? We have to come up with the best Christmas card picture to send to the Crews of Damon's Mountains!"

"Oh. Yes, that seems important." More important than getting along, she supposed. Which was good because Grim and Rhett and Kamp fought all the time.

"Get in. We have Christmas shit to buy."

"W-what kind of Christmas...stuff?"

Juno was busy shoving the piles of holiday cards onto her floorboard to clear off the passenger's seat. "We need three giant candy canes, six twelve packs of Pen15 Juice Beer, sixteen strands of holiday lights, and a baby miniature donkey. I've already called Remi. She's going to figure out the timer on the new camera so we can all be in the picture.

Ash tried not to scrunch up her face as she sat into the seat, but she had concerns. "Umm, Juno?" she asked over the blaring hip-hop version of "Silent Night." "I don't think Grim will take a picture like that. He hates Christmas."

"I've already got a plan for that part."

"You do?"

"Yes. A coupon book of future blow jobs from you."

"What?"

"Bribery, Ash. Take six to twelve for the team so we can get this picture."

"Okay." She still had concerns. "But I do that all the time anyways. It's not really taking one for the team if I like it."

Juno hit the gas and skidded on the ice for a second before the tires caught traction and catapulted them forward. She was wearing the biggest smile Ash had ever witnessed.

"Are you okay?" she asked her friend.

"I just love Christmas now! Everything is so different. Before, I was always rushing in to try and see you and Remi and my family in Damon's mountains for a few days in December and then rushing right back out again. Not anymore! Now we have a real-life Crew, Ash! A real one that won't disappear, and we get to build up holiday traditions like I used to do in the Ashe Crew, how you used to do in the Boarlanders, and Remi used to do in the Gray Backs. This is our holiday moment!"

Now Ash couldn't help but get a little bit excited about the picture. Anything that would distract her from how bad she'd done in that interview. So okay…candy canes and beer and baby donkeys. She was on board.

No matter if she got a job right away or not, she was with the man she loved and she lived in the same trailer park in the same Crew as her best friends.

This was going to be the best Christmas ever.

THREE

The trailer park was too quiet.

Ash scanned the clearing, listening. There was no throaty rumble of the logging equipment up the mountain, no scent of the exhaust from the processor, no country music blaring from Rhett's jobsite. The birds who were stubborn enough to try to wait out winter in these mountains were even silent.

"Something's off," Juno said softly from where she stood next to her car with an armload of letters.

The chills up Ash's spine agreed with Juno's observation. "Is it Vyr?" Ash whispered.

"No. We would smell his smoke, and it would be raining ashes."

The clouds above them were dark, but snow

wasn't even falling right now to have them guess at ashes.

These were the Red Dragon's Mountains, and Grim had told her Vyr came back from time to time to scorch the earth and eat the ashes around the border of his territory, but this deafening silence wasn't the dragon's doing. He wasn't quiet. They would've seen fire by now.

"I'm going to check if Remi is in the brewery." Okay, it wasn't really a brewery that the boys had behind the trailers. More like a shed, but the best damn beer brewed on this side of the country was made right there. Rhett had named it Pen15 Juice, a fact that always made Ash laugh when she thought about it, but not right now. Not when her arm hairs were standing straight up under her jacket and she felt lightning was about to strike.

Inside of her, the bear squirmed in discomfort.

"Remi?" Juno called as they made their way around the trailers toward the shed.

"Are you being a beer wench?" Ash asked, her voice echoing through the silent mountains.

"Ash! Juno!" Remi screamed from the woods. "Help!"

"Oh, my God," Juno murmured, right before she threw the letters up in the air and Changed into her massive grizzly bear.

As the holiday cards rained down like snow on Ash, she gave her own bear her body. Remi was in trouble!

Adrenaline dumping into her bloodstream, Ash landed on all four paws and dug into the snowy earth with her long, curved claws as she bolted after Juno. All she could see from behind Juno was flying snow and bear-butt.

"Ash!" Remi screamed again.

Shoot, shoot, shoot! Maybe the Tarian Pride was here to finish Grim off! Or maybe the council of lion shifters was rebuilding and trying to recruit him! The woods were sailing by now, and it was all she could do to keep up with Juno. Remi's pleading cries for help were rattling around in her head right along with her theories on what the heck could be wrong.

Maybe she'd fallen and broken an ankle, or perhaps one of the boys hurt themselves on one of the dangerous logging machines! Or an avalanche! Or, or, or—

Juno skidded to a stop in the snow so fast Ash ran

right into her and they tumbled end over end until they landed at Kamp's feet. Remi's mate was leaned up against a giant pine tree, arms crossed, twig hanging loosely from his lips, glaring at two brawling lions and one pissed-off she-grizzly trying to stop the fight.

Grim, her scarred-up, fearsome, hellraiser of a mate looked to be successfully murdering Rhett right now. There on the ground was the Christmas hat Ash had given Grim, and the three-way fight between Remi-the-griz and the two lions was so shockingly violent Ash stood up slowly with her big bear mouth hanging open.

What the fuck? she tried to say out loud, but it came out as *grrrrrr*. Then she snuffled at the end. It sounded like a bear-sneeze. Very un-intimidating.

This was fight number four, and it was only Tuesday, the second day of the week. She knew because she was very good at counting and two was a very easy number to count to.

The Reaper was on a fighting spree.

If she wasn't fourteen percent worried about Grim's teeth on Rhett's throat, she would've taken a moment to admire his lithe agility and ability to murder, but as it stood, Rhett was in trouble.

Juno apparently figured that out at the same time Ash did, and they both bolted for the fight.

Kamp still looked uninterested in being a hero, so okay, it was lady-beast time. Girl power, lady prowess, woman speed, and— *Oh, God, Grim was scary when he slapped a claw out like that.* He probably wouldn't hurt her, though, being his mate and all, so she spun away from the claws of destruction and then barreled right into him with her round, furry rump. He fell hard

On his back, Grim sank his front paws into her neck and shoulders before he even looked at her, and as she stood over him, staring into his empty yellow eyes, she regretted, with such clarity, exactly five things she'd done today. One, she'd smeared moisturizer on her toothbrush instead of toothpaste. Two, she brushed her teeth for a good four seconds before she realized it was coconut-flavored and slimy, not minty and crisp. Three, her socks didn't match because she'd forgotten to put her laundry in the dryer last night, and one of them was an ankle sock that kept slipping down to the arch of her foot. That was the big reason she'd been distracted in the interview. Four, she'd agreed to help find a baby donkey, but it wasn't baby donkey season right now and she had concerns about finding baby livestock in the dead of winter and would probably let Juno down. And five, her biggest regret, attacking the danged Reaper, thinking he wouldn't hurt her. His claws were sharp!

She'd already had a weird day and he was making it worse.

Kisses not claws—that's what mates deserved.

So...

She bit him.

Because good men should hear compliments when they did something right, but they also should get their asses handed to 'em when they messed up.

And he was messin' up!

She sank her teeth right into his shoulder, swearing up and down in her mind that she would set the mountains on fire before she gave the Reaper a coupon book for blow jobs.

He extracted his claws, so she let him go as a reward for stopping the hurt. He bellowed a forest-shaking roar and buckled in on himself, thrashing in the snow. And then his lion imploded into a hunky, tattooed, mohawked man-form that was super cute, but also super in trouble.

When she sucked her bear in tight, she yelped at the pain of the quick Change. While she sat there on her knees in the snow, huffing and hurting, she mindlessly yelled, "You're ruining Christmas!"

"What?" Grim groaned, holding his bleeding shoulder.

"It's three days before the best day of the year, and you're fighting with Rhett. Again!"

"Because he's fucking with me," Grim snarled, his bright yellow eyes on Rhett-the-hissing-lion.

When Rhett charged, Ash yelled as loud as she could, holding her hand up to stop him but, luckily, Remi-the-bear neatly swatted his legs out from under him and he smashed onto the snowy ground, chin first.

"How is he messing with you?" Ash asked, baffled about what could possibly have caused her mate to once again fight his own dang Crew.

Grim stood up and dusted snow off his dick. Snow. Off his giant, swinging, perfect dick. *Focus.*

He jammed a finger at Rhett and announced, "He got off his rig and made his way a damn mile to drop a fuckin' Santa hat on my jobsite."

Ash frowned and pointed at the red hat sitting in the snow. "That one?"

"Yep! And he gave me a Goddamn pebble that won't stop talking to me. I'm not sleeping well because I can't shut off the fucking Reaper. I just want to stay steady, but I can't if my own damn Crew is making me feel crazy!"

"You are crazy," Rhett gritted out after he Changed back into his naked man form. He already had one helluva black eye. Eek. They must've had a fist fight before they turned lion and tried to kill each other. Men. "I didn't walk a mile in the snow to drop a stupid hat off to you, you dunce!"

Grim tried to charge, but Ash restrained him by the shoulders. "Call me a dunce again," he challenged Rhett."

"Dunce."

Grim yelled a bellowing noise that echoed across the mountains. But thank the Lord, Kamp finally moved his ass off the tree to help because Ash couldn't have held Grim back for long, and Remi and Juno were still bears.

"I gave you the Santa hat this morning," Ash said.

"Remember?"

A deep frown drew Grim's dark eyebrows down low. As he stared at her with such confusion swimming in those striking gold eyes, she softened her tone. "Well, don't ya? I bought it in town yesterday on sale, half off. I got two of them, one for me, too, and asked you to take a selfie this morning in front of ten-ten to send to my dad. Which you did."

Grim huffed a shocked-sounding breath and staggered back a step. "I did?"

"Crazy."

"Shut up, Rhett!" Grim and Kamp both yelled at the same time.

"Is no one gonna tackle the fact that our Alpha has a talking pebble in his pocket?" Rhett yelled.

Grim's cheeks were red, from pain or exertion maybe, but Ash was real good at reading him, and she thought it was maybe from something else. Shame.

"I just..." he said, letting the words trail off. "I just wanted to..." His face twisted with anger. "Why are you still here?" he asked to no one in particular, and then he turned and strode into the woods without looking back. At the edge of the tree line, he shoved his feet into a pair of toppled work boots. Then he stooped and picked up a pair of discarded jeans on his way into the forest.

Ash was trying to remain serious and focused, but Grim was the hottest man she'd ever seen, and he was naked and had shoulders as wide as the broadside of a barn, tattoos on his back, and muscles everywhere. Every. Where. And an ass you could bounce a quarter off of. She didn't really understand that saying, but lots of people in Damon's Mountains had said it about the males with the muscle butts.

Compliments usually fixed things, so she called out, "Your bottom looks very nice. Very firm. I'm sorry I bit you! Kind of..." She checked, and he hadn't even punctured her skin with his claws. He was upset with himself and confused, and she had a feeling the second lion in her mate, the Reaper, was playing mind games.

She mourned the loss of her shredded clothes for just a moment before she grabbed her wool-lined boots, pulled them onto her feet fast, and jogged through the crunching snow after him.

If he wanted to, Grim could disappear like a ghost, but he'd left tracks in the snow, deep ones like he was moving fast. The wind was strong and cold, and her skin was half-frozen, so it felt like an eternity before she finally saw him. Grim sat on a felled log, his jeans on but unbuttoned, his head in his hands, him rubbing his hair back and forth slowly like he did when he had a headache.

"You thinking?" she asked, closing the distance between then.

His shoulders lifted and fell with his sigh. "Trying to remember." He forced a tired smile. "I don't like Christmas much."

"You don't? Or the Reaper doesn't?"

Grim leaned forward and captured her hand with his, pulled her between his legs and rested his head against her breasts and neck. "You are the cleverest person I've ever met."

"Me? Have you been drinking?"

Grim chuckled warmly, and the sound thawed her skin. There was her man.

"I guess the Reaper doesn't like it much."

"Why not?"

"Because I wasn't allowed to celebrate it after he was born. The council thought holiday sentiment would make me too soft. The Reaper feels the same."

Ash cradled his head and ran her nails through

his hair. "Oh, Grim, I'm sorry." She hated what the council had done to him. Alienated him, made rules that he couldn't have a mate, took his childhood friend, Ronin, away from him, ruined the holidays… They stripped him of joyful moments so he would be molded into the killer the Tarian Pride needed.

The council was all dead now, but that didn't stop her from wishing them back to life so she could maul them all over again. And that was saying something because she was a submissive bear, not a war bear.

"I really love you, you know?" she murmured, scratching his head over and over. "And I really understand you. You're doing good."

Grim huffed a breath and hugged her closer, hiding his eyes from her. "I think you're just supportive. I don't know why, but to you, I can do no wrong. I wanted to bring you back here, put you in 1010, take you on dates and make your heart fall for this place. For me. I wanted to be a better Alpha so I could give you a Crew you'll always be safe in. I wanted to hit logging numbers so Vyr will keep paying us. I wanted to give you a good life."

"And you are."

"No, I'm not. It's not good enough. I'm here,

disrupting work, fighting the Crew instead of leading them, going crazier—"

"You aren't—"

"I am and you know it, Ash." He softened his voice and repeated, "I am."

"Enough," she murmured, cupping his cheeks and lifting those blazing yellow eyes to her. Those were the Reaper's eyes, but Grim sounded like Grim. That said one thing to her. The Reaper was compromising, even if Grim didn't see it that way. "Grim, you push people away. You learned to do that from your time with the Tarian Pride. Anyone you paid attention to got ripped away from you, so this is how you were built. The people you care about the most, you keep your distance so you can keep them."

The emotion fell from his face so fast his ears moved slightly. He looked utterly stunned. "Say that again."

Ash inhaled deeply and stroked his dark beard. "The people you care about the most, you keep your distance from. Because you want to keep us."

Grim turned his head toward the woods fast, but she'd already seen it—the moisture that had built in his eyes. The emotion there. She was breaking him again. Breaking him so she could help him put himself back together.

Sometimes breaking a man was necessary.

"How do I fix that?" he asked, his voice scratchy and deep, thick with pain, the heart kind. She was the only one who could read him like a book, no one else.

"You figure out you're safe with us," she whispered, and then she kissed the top of his head. "And then you own your faults, apologize when you're wrong, reward us for sticking around."

"How?"

"By letting us in. Let your Crew know you. The real you. That's the best Christmas present you could give any of us, Grim. You."

His sigh tapered into a growl, but there was a smile in his voice when he uttered, "All I wanted to do was come here and find a Crew who would put me down, and you're ruining all my plans."

She snickered. "Good. I want to bone you for a hundred years. Sorry, mister, but you're going to have to stick around. You have shit to accomplish."

"You're shivering."

"Well, I'm naked and it's freezing out here."

"But you're a bear."

"Still cold! I was all warm and bundled up in a nice jacket and my favorite skinny jeans that only make me muffin top a little, and you made me rip them up Changing into a bear."

"You didn't have to Change," he pointed out, folding her suddenly into his arms and lifting her like she weighed no more than a holiday ornament. "You could've just let me kill Rhett."

"Does the pebble he gave you really talk?" she asked, wrapping her arms around his bare shoulders.

"You're so fucking cute wearing nothing but snow boots."

"No changing subjects on me."

Grim let off a little growl as he made his way into the woods in the direction of the trailer park. He was getting stompier in the snow as they went along, but she needed to know the level of his crazy so she could accept it all.

"Its name is Rebble the Pebble and it shit-talks to me in Rhett's voice. Currently he's singing Christmas songs, but during the choruses, he sings in fart sounds."

Ash snorted. She didn't mean to! But she couldn't help it. It was kind of funny. "Well, why do you keep carrying it around?"

Grim shrugged his massive shoulders. "I dunno. Sometimes it says funny stuff. And every once in a while it's nice to hear funny stuff instead of the Reaper just repeating the words, 'Kill them' every thirty seconds."

"Reaper!"

Grim snapped those bright yellow eyes right to her, and his pupils pinpointed. "Yes?"

"Stop trying to kill your friends."

"Reaper doesn't have friends."

"False. You have friends and a girlfriend."

"Mate," he corrected.

"Not yet," she said, lifting her chin primly.

Grim narrowed his eyes. "What do you mean?"

"I have zero claiming marks. Only you have one. You're my mate, but I'm still just a girlfriend."

For a moment, his face looked totally feral. Like there was only wild, injured, furious animal there and no man at all. But the twisted snarl faded away in a second, and Grim's eyes faded to a soft brown. "How did your interview go?"

Ash scrunched up her face and hugged his shoulders tighter as he ducked them under a low-hanging branch. "I didn't get the job."

"How do you know?"

"Because I messed up all my words, and she had to keep asking me to repeat myself. She asked me three times what I meant by my answers, and then I got so nervous I mostly thought about my messed-up sock and just looked down at my hands and stopped answering her questions altogether. She told me, 'It was nice to meet you. Good luck with your job-hunt' right before I left."

"It's okay."

"No, it's not. I can't do good at interviews with strangers. I don't understand them."

"But you understand me, and Remi and Juno. Even Rhett and Kamp, and they are both idiots."

"Yeah, but I'm comfortable with the Crew. My thoughts get all jumbled up when I talk to other people. It's always been like that."

"Well, that means it wasn't the job for you. You'll find another—"

"I wanted to buy your grandma a plane ticket here," she blurted out.

Grim stopped right at the edge of the clearing of the trailer park. "What?"

"For Christmas. For your present. I wanted to bring her here so you didn't have to spend a single Christmas away from her."

"But...I always had to spend them away from her. The council gave me jobs on Christmas."

"To keep you tough, they separated you from her. But you aren't in the Tarian Pride anymore. There is no council." She wiggled out of his arms and hugged him up tight, way up on her tiptoes because Grim was a giant. "Year one out of the Tarian Pride, and shits-a-changin'. I wanted to help it turn around even more, but I don't have much room on my credit card, and I don't feel comfortable charging to it when I don't have a job. And now I don't know what to do for you, and I'm going to mess up your first Christmas outside of the Pride."

Grim pressed his lips against hers. He held there for a two-count before he softened his mouth and moved against hers. His tongue brushed her lips, and she opened for him, excitement building in her middle. She would never, ever get tired of kissing this man.

He ran his fingers through her hair, then held her face inches from his. "Just the fact you thought about giving me a good first Christmas and bringing my grandma here is the best present in the world. You really love me, don't you?"

Ash nodded. "Always. Silly man, don't you see? I gave my whole heart to you." She shrugged up her shoulders because she was a shrugger and smiled with her head canted to the side. "I'm here."

His smile stretched slowly across his face and lit up his brown eyes. "And I'm here."

Then his eyes changed to yellow. "Me, too," he said in a demon's voice.

His eyes changed to the green of his nice lion. "Me three."

Grim growled long and low and then gritted his teeth before he said, "Rebble says 'Me four.'"

Ash cracked up. "I like your kind of crazy."

"Dear God, woman, you are the only one in the world who would ever say that."

Another Ash-shrug. "Maybe no one else could handle it, but you're easy to me. We just fit."

"Mmmm," he rumbled, leading her by the hand toward the trailer at the very far end of the park. 1010. "Or maybe you were just built to accept a man like me." He tossed her a quick grin. "Or maybe you just have terrible taste in men."

She smacked his arm, and he laughed.

"Rebble says he agrees. Terrible taste."

"Well, I secured an Alpha of a Crew *and* a trailer park, so who is the real winner?"

Grim snorted as they climbed the stairs of 1010. "Still not you." He squeezed her hand and turned to her right before she reached for the door handle. "Ash?"

"Yes?" she asked, confused at how serious he'd suddenly become.

"I heard you earlier."

"Well...good, because I'm very loud when I talk."

"No, no, I don't mean that. I mean...I paid attention when you told me I need to let the Crew in. I'll do better."

She smiled and leaned up, kissed his lips. "I know," she whispered as she eased away and rested her forehead onto his. "Someday you will be a great Alpha, Grim. You just have some work to do to get there, but I know you can do it. You and the Reaper both. And Rebble. You have people now. Not just a council controlling you. I mean, you have a support system. And I'll be here the whole way, cheering you on and keeping you on track."

"Vyr told me once to create a team of people who care enough to stop me when I go off the rails."

"*Vyr* is off the rails," she pointed out, visions of him burning Tarian Pride Crew territory still fresh in her mind. "But he was right about that."

"Today, you stopped me when I went after Rhett. You even bit me to bring me back, and when you did that, Vyr's words were loud in my head. So…I guess what I'm saying is…thank you. For stopping me."

"Babe, I'm like the Guardian of the Reaper."

Grim chuckled. "Okay that's a cool-ass nickname, but you shouldn't have to take that job on. I have to get better at this."

"Okay!" She was motivated now. She was going to help him and be his biggest cheerleader. "Step one—stop trying to kill everyone."

"And step two?"

She grinned so big, her cheeks hurt. "Believe in Christmas."

FOUR

It felt like Antarctica out here this morning.

Grim swung the ax down again, splitting the log in half so efficiently, both pieces flew off the chopping block. It had to be ten degrees out with this wind chill. Smelled like snow, and the dark clouds above backed that theory. A winter storm would probably open up on them today.

Vyr hadn't sent paychecks since they'd gone to war with his Crew. The Red Dragon owned these mountains and did what he wanted. The Rogue Pride Crew had stopped Vyr from claiming the mountains Grim's grandmother lived in, and now the dragon was pissed. Grim had called him three times, only to be ignored. He was more of a hash-this-shit-out-face-to-face kind of man, but Ash didn't want that. She was afraid the dragon would lose his temper and turn Grim to ash. Ha. Turn Grim to Ash.

"You swing an ax like a girl," Rebble observed unhelpfully from his pocket. Why Grim kept carrying the damned thing, he couldn't figure out. Mouthy little rock. It wasn't even an imaginary friend. It was an imaginary enemy. Who did that?

"Well," he muttered, "I don't know if you noticed, you little shit, but the girls in this Crew are badasses, so I'm gonna take that as a compliment."

"You swing an ax like a *six-year-old* girl."

Grim hated everything.

"Hey, boss?" Rhett said from behind him.

Grim nearly jumped out of his skin and stopped the ax mid swing. "Holy fuck, Rhett! Don't sneak up on a man like that."

"Uh, I tromped over here from my trailer like a limping rhinoceros. You weren't paying attention. Probably thanks to you talking to yourself. Again."

"It's the dumb rock you gave me," Grim muttered, resting the blade of the ax in the snow and leaning against the handle.

Rhett gave a mushy smile that made Grim want to

barf. "I kept mine, too," he said, fishing his own rock out of his pocket. "So I can remember the day we became friends."

Old Grim would've reminded Rhett that he hated him and he didn't have friends, but he really had listened to Ash when she said he needed to let people in.

Rhett popped up the collar of his jacket and zipped it up. "It's cold as fuck out here this morning," he said, taking a seat on the wood pile against Grim's trailer. "Gonna be brutal working today."

"Yeah, well, you aren't getting out of it," Grim grumbled, picking up another log to split.

"I don't want to get out of it."

Grim waited for a punchline, but Rhett just stared at him.

"You know," Rhett said, "the first day we hit our numbers...I don't think I've ever been prouder of myself."

"What? You're a famous musician. You don't need this place or some number on a piece of paper. You're already successful."

"Not true. I didn't see myself as successful until I met Juno. Until I learned what made her happy, until I could work all the machines here, until I could go a whole day without fighting with you or Kamp. My music career? That's temporary. It only takes one mistake, and I'm out of favor in the public eye. And we both know I'll fuck it up sooner or later," he said with a grin.

Grim nodded because, well, he really fuckin' agreed with that.

"But this place is bigger. You know?"

As far away from Rhett as possible, Grim sat on the woodpile and spun the ax blade slowly in the snow, making a little circle. "I don't really know how to do this."

"Do what?" Kamp asked, striding around the side of the trailer with a trio of coffee cups in his hands.

Grim muttered a "thank you" as he took one Kamp offered him. No one had ever brought him coffee before.

"I mean, I don't know how to do any of this."

"Well, there ain't no instructions, but that's the beauty of this Crew," Kamp said, taking a seat beside Rhett. He sipped his coffee and made an "aaaaah" sound, then said, "Every Crew is different. We all accepted a long time ago that we were all gonna fuck this up. And we have. But we're still here, and the girls are happy."

"That matters a lot to me," Grim rumbled.

"It happens when you find the one," Rhett said. "It changes your perspective. You go along living your life selfishly for years and you get in the habit of caring about your comfort, then all of a sudden, you have someone who smiles when you make *them* comfortable. Someone you love. And that becomes more important than yourself."

"Rebble just called you a pussy," Grim said with a snort.

"Really?" Rhett asked.

"No, not really." Grim's sigh tapered into a growl. "He only insults me."

Kamp let off a bellowing laugh. Just one. And then Rhett snickered. And as much as Grim tried not to laugh, too, he couldn't help himself. The three biggest fuck-ups were sitting on a woodpile at five am, cracking up, freezing their balls off, and talking about life like they knew what the hell they were doing. And he was king of the fuck-ups!

Wiping the corners of his eyes, Grim cleared his throat and said, "How about we hit the quota today?

Hit it, and I'll buy you all a beer in town after. We'll bring the girls and get a break from the mountain. Give them a good night."

Kamp and Rhett were just sitting there staring at him. Just...staring. Unblinking. The only movement from them was the steam coming from their coffee cups.

"What?" he growled.

"Did you...?" Rhett whispered. "Did you just invite us to hang out?"

Grim snarled and stood, leaned the ax against the woodpile, and stomped past them. For good measure, he shoved Rhett hard enough in the shoulder that he spilled half of his coffee and then Grim demanded, "Don't be weird about it."

He walked toward his jobsite with a smile on his face.

Not because he cared—

"Liar," Rebble said.

—but because he'd made Rhett spill his coffee.

"You love them, you soft little weenie-boy," Rebble said in a smug voice.

Kill them, the Reaper whispered as usual.

"No," Grim said, but he couldn't for the life of him

tell if he was talking to the Reaper or arguing with the rock in his pocket.

No matter, though. Grim was in a good mood and motivated. He was going to work his ass off today, come home to Ash tonight, and then take her out, because Rhett was right about one thing. Ash's comfort was more important than his. He breathed for her smiles.

She'd said the best Christmas present he could give the Crew was himself. Well, he thought that was insane because he mostly belittled them and tried to murder them, but okay. He would put in the effort and have a night out with the Crew.

And maybe that would make Ash smile a lot.

Soft little weenie-boy? Whatever.

Not even imaginary insults could get to him today.

Grim was a monster on a mission, and that mission was to fuck up a little less today. Sure as shit, he didn't know what he was doing as an Alpha, but his Crew seemed to be fine with a D-minus leader, so there really wasn't that much pressure. Their expectations were non-existent, thanks to him setting the bar exceptionally low.

Grim shrugged and hunkered down into his jacket as he stepped onto the trail that led to the forest he'd been clearing.

Fighting his Alpha rank here hadn't done him any good, so maybe he would try something new now— like failing less.

Why the hell not?

FIVE

"Oh, good, now hell has frozen over, too," Remi murmured.

Maybe it really had. Ash stared dumbfounded at the trio of giants who strode through the snow. Grim was up front but only by a few paces, and Kamp and Rhett were at his flanks. They looked exhausted, half-frozen, but all three of them were matching. With smiles.

"Whaaaat the heeeeell?" Juno whispered from where she was draping holiday lights around the porch railing of 1010. "Y'all are seeing this, too...right?"

"Does it look like friendship?" Ash asked.

"Yep," Remi said from where she sat crisscross

applesauce on the bright red plastic lawn chair Ash
had dragged onto the porch.

"Then yes. I see it, too."

"Maybe they're playing a prank," Juno theorized.

When Ash looked at her friends' faces, they were
matching, too, with suspicious, squinty eyes. Ash
believed in the boys, though. Sure, they liked to try to
kill each other, but they could also be friends.

She and the girls had been setting up the perfect
holiday picture right in front of 1010, complete with
cases of Pen15 Juice on the porch and bright holiday
lights all over the singlewide trailer, and a trio of
giant candy canes propped up against the porch.
They'd tried really hard to track down a baby donkey
to put some reindeer antlers on, but had failed. None
of the neighbors would even let them borrow a tame-
ish cow. Two had told them they knew Rogue Pride
was full of shifters and didn't want their livestock
eaten. Juno had hung up dramatically both times and
then said she was going to go eat a cow from each of
their herds on principle, but she was also on her
period and a little grumpy. She wouldn't really do
that. Probably.

It was okay, though, because Kamp's son Raider

got to visit a couple weekends before the war with the Sons of Beasts, and he and Remi had knitted a little Santa suit for their pet naked mole rat named Waffles with Peanut Butter. Waffles for short. Remi currently had the hideous little critter bundled in her jacket to keep it warm for the picture, but the thing had bitten her six times already. Ash was good at counting. That bald little rodent was very angry inside. But Ash liked her. Waffles reminded her of Grim, and she thought Grim was very cute, even when he was bitey and grumpy. They should've named her Reaper Junior instead of Waffles with Peanut Butter. Just thinking about waffles made her tummy growl.

Grim was so hot in his work jeans, scuffed-up boots, wool-lined jacket undone to expose a red and black flannel underneath, and gray beanie covering his mohawk. He was tall and strong as an oak, long powerful strides, arms busting against the seams of his jacket, ax in his hand. This was like one of those movie scenes where a big mountain man was coming in from a blizzard like the cold weather didn't affect him at all. Or like when a hero walked away from an explosion without flinching. All three of the boys looked so cool. Until Kamp turned and kicked Rhett's ankle mid-stride, and he tripped and fell face-first in the snow. He cussed a lot so Kamp kicked more snow on him and cackled like a hyena. And then Grim told them they were both worthless. But before *that*, they looked very cool.

The second Grim looked up and caught her eye, Ash took off. She didn't want to not be touching him for another second, so she bolted through the snow and leapt through the air as he held his arms out. She wasn't one of those skinny girls, but she had faith in her man to catch her. And catch her, he did. His chuckle was deep, growly, and sexy, and he nipped her neck immediately as she hugged him up tight. Goodness, she loved this man. He smelled so good, so familiar, like home.

"I missed you all day," she announced much too loudly against his ear. Grim hunched his shoulders, so she said, "Sorry, I'm just excited to see you."

He eased her back onto her own feet in the snow and kissed her so sweetly she knew what color his eyes were not. The Reaper must've been sleeping because he didn't allow gentleness. His eyes would be the brown of his human side or the green of the good lion.

"I love you I love you I love you," she murmured, rubbing her nose against his.

"Sweet mate," he rumbled, hugging her tighter.

"Get a room," Rhett groused as he stomped by.

"How was your day?" she asked Grim, ignoring grumpy Rhett.

He heaved a frozen sigh and said, "Better now. It was long and so fuckin' cold up there, but the boys did good and we hit our numbers." He grinned but ducked his face from her fast.

"You're proud," she sang softly.

"Hell, yeah, I am. We rarely have good work days. I didn't fight anyone today. And no one made excuses to quit early." He cleared his throat and his eyes grew serious. "I'll have to give the Reaper the body tonight, though."

"I'll Change with you." She cupped his cheeks and grinned at him. "Grim, I'm proud of you."

He snorted. "Woman, you say that if I lower the toilet lid after a piss."

Ash shrugged. It was true. He'd been a bachelor for so long that she fell into the toilet in the middle of the night once because the lid was up. Now he always tried to lower it. Heck yeah, she was so proud!

"I have a question," he murmured. "A couple questions, actually."

Oh, that sounded very serious. "Okay. I'm ready."

"One, do you want to go on a date with me tonight? And the Crew. A Crew date. I owe the boys a beer."

"Gasp!" she exclaimed. "Yes! What are we going to do?"

"Well, we have to drive a shipment of logs down to the lumberyard, but I figured we could all pile in and go to that tourist bar right off that little mountain road that leads into town."

"Meaties on the River?"

He laughed and gave one nod. "Yup, that's the one."

"Yes! I want to date there. Crew date. I mean, I want to do that. I mean, let's do a date there."

"Good. And two," he said, his eyes dancing. He was the most handsome man in the whole world when he smiled like this. "Do you want to register to be my mate?"

Ash froze. Just…her body stopped working or feeling or responding. Even her lips. In her head, she was thinking, *Yes, Grim, I would love to register to be your mate for all the public to see.* But all that came out when she forced the words was, "Waffles is a bad rat."

"Agreed," Grim said, dropping his chin to his chest. "Did you hear what I just said?"

Ash tried and failed to inhale a deep breath. Did the oxygen disappear from the mountains? Breathing was like sucking on a vacuum right now, and her lungs were screaming. Finally, she wheezed out, "Yes!"

Her eyes were burning. Or freezing. She got embarrassed because she didn't like people seeing her all weak and crying, so she buried her face against the impossibly sturdy indention between his pecs.

"Are you okay?" he asked. "You're shivering." He wrapped her into his open jacket. "Are you cold?"

"Nope, I shake when I cry. Don't think that's lame and leave me."

"Woman, I just asked you to register to me and the Crew. As my mate. I'm not going anywhere."

"But you never bit me, so I was confused. Sometimes when you're gone all day, I think maybe you don't like me enough to bite me, and then I get embarrassed that I bit you first because I think it's supposed to be the boy who does it first, but my bear just did it and I thought I messed everything up and—"

"Aaaash," he crooned, gripping her by the arms and easing her crying, tear-soaked, sobby, make-up smeary face away from his chest to look at her. Great, there was mascara all over his shirt.

He ran his thumbs under her eyes and cupped her cheeks. "I'm scared to bite you because of the Reaper, Ash. I don't want to hurt you more than I have to when I claim you. I've been waiting for him to settle down. You think I don't want to give you a claiming mark? I stay awake every night you spend in my bed thinking about it. I want you bound to me. I just don't think the Reaper can be trusted with something like that. Not yet. This paperwork would announce to the whole world that you are mate of Grim and member of the Rogue Pride Crew, though. The whole Crew is registering—"

"Not me," Rhett called from where he was scraping his boot off on the bottom stair of 1010. "I hate you all today."

"He's just hungry," Juno called out. "Carry on. None of us are listening!"

Ash could barely make out Kamp whisper-scream, "Rhett, shut the fuck up."

Grim glared at the Crew, all milling about the front of the trailer, trying to look busy but not really doing anything. Remi was just plugging and unplugging the Christmas lights and Juno was inspecting the snow on the porch railing.

Grim muttered a very bad cuss word under his breath and pulled Ash by the hand back toward the woods, farther away from the Crew. "So I guess what I'm asking is for you to be mine, but to be patient because our mating story will just have to be a little different than other pairs."

"Like no claiming mark," she said.

Grim's smile was tiny and sad. "I wish I could do just one thing normal, Ash. I want to give you the world, and you deserve for our pairing to be exactly the way you want it."

"No." Ash lifted her chin, planted her feet, and crossed her arms. "I don't want that. I don't want the same story as everyone else because you are different and I am different, and together we are different. And that's okay. Yes, I want to ride in the log truck and help you drop off the lumber and eat and drink at Meaties on the River with you and my other four best friends—"

"Don't forget to include Waffles!" Rhett called.

"My five best friends," Ash corrected. "And, yes, I want to register to our Crew and to you. And then you'll be mine and I'll be yours and we will officially bang for the rest of our lives. Whatever we decide to do with claiming is our business and is perfect for us. You aren't doing anything wrong. You're protecting me."

"You really see me, don't you?" he asked softly.

"Yes, and I love everything you are. Reaper and all. I'm an accepter, remember?"

"You're perfect, Ash."

"Oh no, not me. I'm a mess."

"Not to me. Your mess is beautiful. To me, you're the perfect match."

She giggled. "I'm not a match, silly. I'm a girl."

He belted out a laugh and swatted her ass, guided her back toward the Crew. "I didn't mean a match that you light. I meant someone who fits me."

"Oh. Yes, I fit you very good." She waggled her

eyebrows so he would know she meant it in a perverted way but every time she did, her nose flared uncontrollably, so she probably looked weird. But he didn't look concerned about her facial health. He just chuckled a lot. And that was a victory, because when she'd first met Grim, he had very, very little laughter in his life. And now that happy sound came easy. A big part of her hoped she had something to do with that.

A good man deserved laughs. Grim had The Bad in him, sure, but The Good was way bigger.

SIX

This picture was going really wrong.

Click.

The camera was on a tripod and the timer was set to take pictures at intervals.

Grim growled low in his throat, and Ash could feel the sickening waves of dominance buzzing off him.

"Maybe don't stand that close to Grim," she whispered to Rhett, shoving him back a couple feet from where he hovered on Grim's left-hand side.

"I'm his best friend. I should be the one standing next to him."

"How are you his best friend?" Kamp asked around the candy cane hanging from his lips. He puffed it like a cigar and then spoke as he blew smoke into the air, "You have a giant black eye from where he punched your face yesterday, and he deemed you *last* in the Crew."

Click, went the camera.

"Sixth in the Crew. Sixth!" Rhett said before he took another swig of homemade beer.

Grim was growling louder now. "Is this almost done?"

"I want one good picture, and you idiots have been talking in every one," Juno said, striking another fashionable pose with her leg extended and her hand on her hip. She was wearing elf shoes with bells hanging off the curved toes and the reindeer antlers they'd gotten for the baby donkey. Her shoes looked very uncomfortable and cold.

Kamp was holding mistletoe over Remi's head while she pretended to kiss Waffles. Suddenly, Remi flinched back. "Owwww, you bit me, you bald little fu—"

Click.

"You forgot your hat," Rhett said unhelpfully as he handed Grim the Santa hat they'd fought over yesterday. "Kamp would have never remembered your costume. My Christmas wish is that you make him be Sixth and make me Fifth."

Click.

"Your eyes are really yellow," Ash whispered. "Like the Grinch's."

"Kamp, get off your phone," Juno demanded.

"I'm taking a selfie," he muttered, aiming the phone at him, Remi, Remi's bleeding lip, and Waffles, who looked a little bit like a penis dressed in a Santa costume. A penis with teeth.

Juno shoved Kamp hard in the shoulder.

Click.

"Hey! You made the picture all blurry!" he griped, glaring at his camera screen.

"Yeah?" Juno said in a dangerously low voice. She jammed a finger toward the camera. "What about the actual picture we are supposed to be taking for the Christmas card?"

"It's two days before Christmas, Juno," Grim gritted out, staring with dead yellow eyes at the camera. "How can we even send these out in time?"

"I've compiled an email list!"

"Oh, my God, I just found a candy bar in my pocket," Kamp announced. "Here, Rhett, feed it to your mate quick. She's on her period."

"Don't be a dick!" Rhett shoved Kamp hard who knocked into Remi who gave a scary-sounding bear growl.

Click.

A long, feral shriek came from Juno. "I've asked for zero things from this Crew. Zero! All I wanted was a good picture to send to the Crews of Damon's Mountains because I'm proud of us! I'm proud we ended up here!"

While Juno was yelling at the Crew, Grim pulled on his Santa hat, scooped Ash in his arms and gave the biggest, most empty, cheesy grin she'd ever seen. Okay. So Ash made the same face at the camera and did a thumbs up. On Grim's other side, Rhett went down hard on account of Kamp tackling him, and Juno was throwing candy canes at them like little mint-scented javelins. Remi was frowning at the camera and holding a squirming Waffles as far away from her body as possible.

Click.

"And that's a wrap," Grim snarled, setting Ash on her feet. He strode right over to the camera and turned it off.

"What do you mean that's a wrap?" Juno asked, a pair of candy cane grenades clenched in each fist. "Those were all terrible!"

Rhett Changed into his lion and then so did Kamp, and now they were roaring and growling and brawling like they wanted to end each other's lives.

Grim blinked tiredly at them and said, "Our Crew is terrible. Those pictures are accurate." He strode off toward his trailer on the other side of the park, his warm, strong hand wrapped around Ash's.

Juno scoffed and called out behind them, "I'll have you know I believe we are a mighty Crew!"

"Weeell," Ash drawled, smiling at Juno sympathetically over her shoulder to try to be supportive. "We are an acceptable Crew. That's pretty good!"

With her bottom lip poked out, Juno sat down hard on a case of Pen15 Juice and pulled one of the beers out. She popped the top just before Ash turned back around to watch where she was going. A beer would make Juno feel right as rain. Kamp brewed the best beer. Rhett and Kamp probably wouldn't kill each other, and Remi was back to trying to cuddle the rat, so everything was fine.

"Meet at the truck in fifteen!" Grim demanded, and a wave of something unfamiliar blasted through his words and straight into her. All she could think about was she needed to be at that truck in fifteen. *Needed to be.*

When she looked back again, the lions had stopped fighting, and both of them were looking at Grim with wide eyes and their mouth's hanging open. Rhett was on his back and Kamp had his paw jammed against his throat, but they'd just stopped mid-brawl to pay attention.

"Babe," she whispered.

"I need your panties around your ankles."

"Ohhhh, okay! But Grim," she tried again.

"Yeah?"

"You just did an Alpha order."

"What? No, I didn't. Those morons will ignore it and be at the truck in an hour if I'm lucky."

"My bear is chanting 'fifteen minutes, fifteen minutes'... Oh, wait. Now 'fourteen minutes, fourteen minutes.' She's very good at counting."

He spun and picked her up, wrapped her legs around his hips and growled, "God, I love you, my little nerdy girl," as he climbed the porch stairs of his trailer with her.

"Me? A nerdy girl? I'm dumb as a post, mister."

"False and not true. You are the smartest girl I've ever met in my life."

"I barely passed high school."

"A pass is a pass."

"I got mostly Ds."

He set her down inside his cabin and pulled at the deep V in her bright red sweater. "I only care about these Ds."

"Double Ds, technically."

"Mmmm, double better," he murmured in a gritty voice, easing her backward into the dark living room.

He shoved her red bubble jacket off her shoulders and dropped it to the floor. *You're supposed to be dressing for the truck like your Alpha ordered you*, her bear enlightened her. *Not undressing.*

Grim's fingertips brushed just underneath the hem of her sweater at both hips. 'Take that off,' she'd meant to say, but her words came out, "Thirteen minutes."

"Plenty of time," he rumbled. "I'll have you coming on my dick in five."

Her heart was pounding against her sternum, and

her body was catching fire from the inside out. Oh, when that man touched her. His lips pressed onto hers in the exact moment the backs of her knees hit the edge of his bed, and she sat down with a gasp. Kisses for her lips and then underneath her jaw, her neck, right behind her ear. He pulled her sweater off smoothly and threw it against the wall. Grim didn't even bother unhooking her bra. He just pushed the cups down until her full breasts spilled out of the top. And there were his hands, massaging her until she tingled. With his knee, he spread her legs and then cupped his big strong hand between her thighs. Ash couldn't help it—she moaned his name because she knew what was coming. She flattened the palm of her hand onto the seam of his jeans. If bears could purr, she would be doing that right now. His thick, swollen cock was pushing against the material there. Breath shaking with her need, she unsnapped the button and pulled the zipper down, then shoved his clothes down his thighs.

Grim's kisses got rough, and his tongue plunged into her mouth, stroking hers. The growl in his throat was wild and uncontained. *Hello, Reaper.* He always came out when Grim was riled up.

Hand on her throat, he gently pushed her backward until her shoulder blades rested on the bed. He left his hand there, but when he squeezed, it was so tender, she barely felt it. Just enough to let her know he wanted to be boss today. She loved when he went dominant like this. The submissive part of her reveled in the fact that her mate was an unapologetic titan in life and in the bedroom. With his free hand, he yanked her leggings and panties down to her ankles. And then that hand was right back on her sex, kneading and rubbing until she was writhing under his touch. Oh, God, she could finish just like this. His finger slid smoothly into her, and then a second finger. She dug her nails into his back and rocked her hips against his hand.

"You always get so wet for me," he murmured against her ear. "Good girl."

Mmmmmm, she loved when he called her that. It was the nickname he'd given her the first time they'd met. But now, in the bedroom, she liked when he told her she was doing something right.

As he moved into position right between her inner thighs, she spread her knees out wider so she could take him. He was so big and powerful, and her

64

body still needed to get used to his size.

He pushed the head of his cock into her and eased out, then in a little farther and eased back out. When she gasped with pleasure, he gripped her hips and pushed into her deep. "Ooooooh," she moaned as he filled her just right.

He pulled back slow and then slammed into her again. Ash closed her eyes as he kissed her, flying high on sensation alone. She wanted only to *feel* what he was doing to her body right now. He pushed into her again and again, faster each thrust.

"Yes, yes, yes."

He stayed deep and bucking shallow, hitting her clit fast, over and over. He was loud with her now, groaning against her sensitive ears as if he was close, too, and as soon as the tingling pressure between her legs became too much, he shoved into her hard and froze, his dick throbbing as she came with him. Over and over, he pulsed with her, their bodies keeping pace, shattering together. Being with him felt like nothing else in the world. This right here, this connection with the man she loved, was everything.

Grim began to move inside of her slowly, drawing out every remaining vibration of her orgasm until she was sated and could only hold onto him and rub his back.

Eight minutes, her inner animal enlightened her.

Ash giggled. "You did it. Five minutes and you made me come."

"Woman, I made us both come. I think that's the fastest I've ever gone."

She laid little kisses all over his beard. "Good dick," she murmured. "Good boy."

"Oh, God," he muttered, laughing. He pulled out of her gently, kissed her once more, thoroughly, and then made his way into the bathroom.

He liked to get moving right after sex, but Ash always laid there like a happy little blob to recover.

Seven minutes.

"Okay, okay," she muttered under her breath, pushing up on the bed. She got a glimpse of herself in the dresser mirror and nearly toppled over laughing. Her cheeks were flushed, her hair was like a rat's nest piled up on top of her head, and her boobs were still hanging out of the top of her bra. She was definitely going to need the entire seven remaining minutes to make herself presentable again.

She grinned at her reflection.

She had zero regrets.

SEVEN

Driving in a blizzard wasn't Ash's favorite. And working at the lumberyard to help the boys unload the logs wasn't the best either. She and Juno and Remi stayed bundled up in the front bench seat of the truck with a blanket over their legs while Grim worked a crane with a claw to put each log they'd cut into the right-sized piles in the yard. Kamp and Rhett were out there, too. Kamp was talking to the owner of the yard, negotiating pay, which went straight back to Vyr's account, and Rhett was standing beside the crane talking into a walkie-talkie to Grim to guide his work.

It was the day before Christmas eve and almost closing time, so the other workers had already gone home. Ash would never get over how sexy it was that her mate could operate any machine he wanted. He was one of those mechanically-minded men who picked up hard labor quickly. He was really good at his job. God, she hoped she could find one soon, too.

Grim parked the crane on the edge of the loading area and hopped out of the rig. He disappeared for a minute in the blustering snow, but he and the boys came back, waving at the foreman and calling out, "You have a Merry Christmas, too."

Grim had just wished someone a Merry Christmas. Huh.

Ash waved out the window at him, but he probably couldn't see her. The snow storm was getting bad. Good thing Meaties was right up the road, not even a mile from here.

Grim and the boys climbed in. There wasn't much room, so Ash had to stay squished up against Grim's ribs (she didn't hate that part at all) and Remi and Juno sat on their mates' laps. They were all bundled up in winter coats and mittens and beanies and snow boots. The girls had all worn bright colors. Ash thought they looked cute for Crew date night, and apparently so did Juno because she opened her window to get a good angle with her phone and told everyone to smile. And then she took a selfie and showed it to Ash. They were all piled in the cab of the logging truck, grinning ear to ear, except for Grim, who had yellow eyes and was only smiling a little. But it was a smile, and for the Reaper, all smiles counted. And good men deserved to know when they looked handsome, so she told him.

"Reaper," she whispered as he pulled onto the narrow two-lane mountain road.

"Mmm?" he rumbled.

"I think you are so cute."

He took his eyes off the road for just a moment, but she saw a flash of something in his expression. Her tiny compliment had touched him. There was softness in the Reaper's eyes.

Happy as a little clam, she slid her arms around his bicep as he maneuvered the big truck along the winding road in the snowfall. Happy as a little clam. What did that saying even mean? Were clams happier than other animals? She imagined clams had bad days, too. Maybe she should say, "Happy as a little Ash Bear" in her head from now on so it would make more sense. Because she was very, very happy.

Her phone vibrated in her pocket as Grim was parking the truck in a row of empty parking spots right in front of Meaties. When she opened the text from her dad, Bash, she couldn't help the smile on her face.

Hey Nugget. Juno just sent me this picture.

The selfie of all of them in the truck showed up in the message.

I don't think I've ever seen you look so happy. I'm proud of you.

For what? she typed out. Send.

For going and getting the man and the life you deserve. I love you. Call us on Christmas. I'm showing this to your mom. She will probably cry. But the happy kind. She does that a lot. It's a little terrifying, but I'm tough about it.

And lately, Ash understood Mom better because she did the same—cried about happy things. Tears weren't always for sadness, she'd learned. Sometimes they were just little eyeball dewdrops of joy.

I love you too, Dad. Merry the-day-before-Christmas-Eve. Send.

Juno and Remi were leaned all the way over, blatantly ogling her phone, both looking super-mushy

71

when she put it back in her pocket. They didn't even pretend they hadn't been reading her texts. Shameless.

"And I love you little snoopers, too," she whispered, bumping Remi's shoulder before ducking her gaze so they didn't see how fiery her cheeks were getting.

When Grim shoved open his door, a gust of snowy wind blew right in. Geez, it was cold! He got out and offered his hand to help her down. And, oh, she'd meant it when she'd told the Reaper he was cute. Tonight, Grim was wearing his nicest work boots, wrangler jeans with no holes at the knees, and a navy-blue sweater that hugged his broad shoulders and tapered at his trim waist. He'd gelled his hair all messy and sexy. At his thick throat, he wore a simple, thin, black leather necklace he told her his grandma had gotten him the last Christmas before the Reaper was born.

She slipped her hand into his and stepped down onto the slick railing before hopping out into the snow drift by the truck like an excited bunny rabbit. He straightened her bright red beanie with the pink pom-pom, swatted her butt to get her going, and then shut the door. Three steps later, his fingertips were resting lightly on her back, like he didn't like going too long without touching her.

She *love* loved him.

Everyone was chattering and happy as they made their way to the bar in the back. Up front were nice tables with real lit candles and holly bouquets. This place was small, but clean and homey, and it was all dark wood and lots of windows. Beyond the far wall, she could see the riverbank, but not much more thanks to the snowfall. This was probably a tourist bar during the warm months, but not tonight. There were a only a few tables full, but she didn't pay attention to them. Juno was telling the Crew about the Christmas the three of them snuck out of their trailers and met up at midnight to try to catch Santa. Except they all fell asleep in the old treehouse Beaston had made and hadn't woken up until the next morning. They were eight years old at the time, and their parents had thrown a friggin' fit when they'd discovered their beds empty at dawn. Ash had been grounded for a whole week for scaring her parents.

She was cracking up as she took a seat between

Grim and Remi. Kamp was on Remi's other side, and beside Grim was Rhett then Juno.

"What can I do you for?" asked a bartender with the name Ralph on his nametag.

"Hey, Layla says that sometimes," Ash pointed out.

"Whose Layla?" Ralph asked.

"She's my favorite bartender back in Saratoga. Sorry. Y-you... Oooh." Ash ducked her head and wrung her hands.

"Go on, girl. You're doing fine," Grim murmured, squeezing her thigh.

Ash inhaled deep and told the bartender, "You probably didn't need to know all that."

"I don't mind," Ralph said with a friendly grin. "It's a slow night. Y'all are the liveliest bunch I've had in here."

"W-what specials do you have?" Ash asked, sitting up straighter. She could see Grim's cheeks swell with a grin beside her, but if she looked at him, she would get distracted and lose her nerve. Talking to people was good. "We're sure hungry, and we've never been here before." She swallowed hard and formed the words in her head carefully. "What's good to eat?"

Ralph was an older gentleman with a receding hairline and glasses and the kindest blue eyes she'd ever seen. He kinda looked like a short-haired, non-bearded Santa. He was even wearing a bright red sweater with little reindeer on it. "Are you those shifters that live up the mountain? The Rogue Pride Crew?"

Ash looked at Grim, but he only nodded in encouragement.

"Yes, sir."

"Call me Ralph. Please." He leaned forward, his eyes twinkling. "I'm pro-shifter. I was sure happy to hear you all moved to these parts. You are the talk of the town."

Ash grinned at her lap. She needed to look up and keep better eye contact. Ralph was nice and not intimidating.

"We got fried catfish baskets on special tonight for half off, and the first round of shots is on me, so long as you let me pick the ones I give you."

Ash looked down the bar both ways at the grinning Crew and then nodded to Ralph. "Deal."

They all ordered catfish baskets and chatted with Ralph while he made shots that were red and green

Christmas colors. He lined them up green, red, green, red, green, red, and then Juno took another selfie of the Crew with Ralph. Ash's best friend sure liked taking a lot of pictures now. Maybe because Juno was really happy to have a Crew to belong to. The longer Ash spent with Rogue Pride, the more she understood the members, her friends, and that was a big deal because people had always been hard for her to understand. Not Grim, though. Never Grim. He had been a perfectly readable book from the first minute she talked to him.

Grim slid a red shot to her and murmured, "To match your pretty hair." Then he lifted a green one up, which matched his pretty green eyes, and said, "To us. Mess. Friends. Crew. We are what we are."

That was about the mushiest Grim got. Rhett made a clicking sound behind his teeth and murmured "awwww" beside Grim.

So Grim punched him in the dick. Rhett hunched in on himself and wheezed. Juno patted his back comfortingly, and the rest of them took their shots like nothing had happened...because Grim was right.

Messy or not, they were what they were.

"Christmas wish time," Remi said as Ralph and

the cook settled the catfish baskets in front of them.

"Pass," Grim muttered. "Can we get a round of beers?" he asked Ralph. "For them, not me. I'm driving. And also I'm a psychopath, so booze isn't the best idea."

Ralph's bushy gray brows lifted. "Fair enough. I appreciate your honesty. Five beers coming up. What do you guys like?"

"Pen15 Juice," Rhett said around a bite.

"Well, I've heard of it, but haven't had the pleasure of working out a deal with the brewer quite yet."

Rhett pointed to Kamp. "Talk to that one before we leave then, and I can deliver what you need after Christmas for a trial run."

Ralph sure looked happy about that, and as he went to check on the other tables at the front of the bar, Remi said a little louder, "I'm serious. Let's hear them. What are your Christmas wishes?" She put her phone on the counter. It said 10:09, but changed right then to 10:10. "Better do them quick!" She put her finger on the number and said, "I hope we get to see Raider again soon."

Kamp put his finger on the number and said,

"Same. Now that my cub is in my life, holidays are a little harder without him." Kamp scooted the phone past Remi to Grim, but he shook his head and passed it right on to Ash. "I hope I get a job soon and Grim's Grandma Rose can come to Christmas."

Rhett was next. "I hope I get a blow job tonight."

Juno swatted his arm and snorted, but pushed her finger on the number quick. Thirty seconds left. Ash was counting. "I hope this year Rhett and I get to start making a family."

"Wait!" Rhett said, his eyes going round. "You want a cub with me?"

Juno nodded. Twenty seconds left.

"I take mine back!" Rhett exclaimed. He put his finger back on the number and said, "I hope I knock up Juno with, like, six cubs this year. I want a hockey team."

"I don't think that's how it works," Kamp pointed out.

"Whatever, *Kamp*. It's my Christmas wish. Fuck off." Rhett shoved the phone to Grim again.

Ten seconds.

Grim looked at the Crew. Eight seconds. He sighed. Seven...Six...

He put his finger on the glowing 10:10 and said, "I hope I can be a better Alpha for all of you." There was an emotional and joyous pause in the Crew. But then Grim said, "And Rebble wishes my dick and balls were smaller so he wasn't so squished in my pocket all the time."

Rhett had been taking a drink of the beer Ralph had just placed in front of him, but choked on the sip and snorted at Grim's revelation. Juno patted his back as he coughed and laughed and coughed and laughed. Really, they were all laughing.

Ralph put a stack of papers in front of Ash, but she didn't understand what they were. "What's this?" she asked.

Ralph pointed to the front window. There was a big sign that said, *Now Hiring*. "I need help around here. You won't be a millionaire working here, but there's benefits and steady hours. And if you're the shy type, which I'm betting you are, it'll be good practice talking to people. Fill that out and bring it back here after the holidays if you're interested. We'll do an interview."

"Really?" she whispered, her stomach fluttering with hope.

"Really. You seem like good people. You shifters have never been handed anything. You earn everything you've got. I bet you would do just fine here."

"I used to sell barbecue. At my last job, I mean."

"Already got food service experience, another bonus."

"Thank you," she uttered, folding the application so she could fit it into her purse. "I mean...thank you for even considering me."

Ralph gave her another really nice smile and patted the bar top. "It was a good wish. A hard worker's wish. I like it." And then he headed back through the kitchen door and disappeared from sight.

"Oh my gosh, oh my gosh, oh my gosh!" she squeaked out, staring in shock at the folded application. She was going to get this job. She had a feeling. She was going to come in here and do soooo good at the interview.

The Crew was gripping her shoulders and congratulating her and telling her she would do well. They said they were proud of her, and she could tell they really were. Their shining eyes and the honest notes in their voices said as much. And Grim wore her very favorite smile.

Today was Ash's new favorite day ever. Her favorites tended to be when the Crew was getting along. Why? Because it was rare. They had to fight for moments like these. That was the nature of a Last Chance Crew. The males in Rogue Pride came with layers and complicated pasts and animals that didn't stay in control. But they all stuck together, even through the bad times. Even through the days when they loved each other but didn't *like* each other.

They fought to stay a Crew because happy moments like this existed. These times tasted sweeter because they were harder to come by.

Ash loved Grim with her whole heart, but he'd given her something he didn't realize yet. He'd given her a Crew to fall in love with, too. This was the first Christmas of many to come. She bet next year, the day before the day before Christmas, this would be their tradition. Meaties on the River and Christmas wishes at 10:10.

And as she looked over her shoulder at the quiet man she'd felt watching them this whole time, she wondered if he would be a part of the tradition, too. The Rogue Pride Crew was laughing and talking around her, not paying attention, but she gave a little two-fingered wave to the dragon in the darkest corner and mouthed, *Merry day-before-Christmas-Eve, Vyr.*

Vyr gave her a smile. It was only a little one, and it didn't reach his eyes. It looked a bit sad even, but it was a smile nonetheless. And for a beast like the Red Dragon, all smiles counted.

Vyr set a wad of money onto the small two-seater table he'd been sitting at and then walked out the side door right next to him.

As she watched him out the window, disappearing into the snowstorm, Grim leaned over and kissed her temple. He whispered, "I'm going to go talk to him."

Oooh. She shouldn't be surprised that her mate knew all along that Vyr was here.

"No more burns," she murmured, tracing the faint scars down the side of her mate's neck.

Grim squeezed her leg and stood. "I'll be right back. Don't let Rhett eat my food."

She wanted to ask if he wanted her to come, too. Heck, her bear wanted to go just to protect Grim. But sometimes a man needed to handle tough situations on his own. And Grim wasn't just a man. He was an Alpha. He'd made a Christmas wish, and here was the beginning. He had to learn how to deal with other Alphas of other Crews. Even the ones he'd gone to war with. She could read Grim real good, and that's what he needed with Vyr.

EIGHT

Grim pushed his way out the door and into the frigid, snowy wind. He couldn't see where Vyr had gone, but he had a feeling the Red Dragon hadn't come all the way here just to sit in the corner of a bar and leave without saying anything. And he sure as hell didn't come here to finish Grim off. If that dragon had wanted him dead, Grim would already be ashes.

They had unfinished business.

Grim shoved his hands into his pockets and gripped Rebble. The snarl in his throat steadied right along with the Reaper. He could barely see ten feet in front of him, but he could make out the man leaning against the back of the logging truck.

"You didn't answer any of my calls," he greeted

Vyr.

The red-haired man twitched his head like a tic, and then he lifted his silver eyes with those elongated pupils to Grim. "I like talking face-to-face."

Vyr felt off. The air around him felt denser and smelled of smoke, but it was more than that. Vyr felt heart sick. Or head sick maybe. The closer Grim got to the monster, the more his animals drew up and prepared to Change. Both of them, The Good and The Bad. And that was bad news for Grim, so he stopped right on the edge of where he could see Vyr and hoped he could keep his skin long enough to have this talk. "I respect that," he murmured. "I like settling things man-to-man, too."

Vyr crossed his arms and said, "I heard your wish in there."

"Congratulations. You have ears."

Vyr huffed a breath and gave a smile that chilled Grim's blood. It was like watching a Tyrannosaurus Rex grin. He lifted two fingers and flicked them slightly. Suddenly, the snow that fell between them disappeared. Grim looked in shock at the clear sphere around them where no snow fell.

"It's like an anti-snow-globe," Vyr murmured.

Fuck, he was much more powerful than anyone realized. He wasn't just a dragon, which was dangerous enough. He was more.

Kill him, the Reaper whispered.

"I wasn't completely decided if I would fire your entire Crew for growing the balls enough to face me in Tarian Pride Territory. It's very hard to pull me off a hunt, and you forced my hand. My dragon doesn't like you."

"Well, none of me likes you, so we're pretty fuckin' even."

Vyr chuckled. "The man in me respects you though. Or maybe I just recognize you. One shitty Alpha to another, I like what you said in there—about wanting to be better. Your mate and your Crew deserve it." He shook his head slightly again, the same tic. "So do mine."

"The Tarian Pride just needs time to rebuild, you know? They have a new lion trying to fix them."

"Ronin won't fix anything. You and I both know it."

Grim gritted his teeth and kicked a snow drift with the toe of his boot. "I believe in him."

"You don't know him. Not anymore. He isn't the

same boy you grew up with. That Pride went after people I consider mine. And like I said, it's very hard to pull my dragon off a hunt." Warning flashed in his bright silver dragon eyes. "Stay out of it, Grim."

The snow began falling between them again so hard Grim could barely see Vyr anymore.

The dragon stood and turned to walk away, but hesitated. For a few seconds, he just froze there with his back to Grim. "Bash sent me a picture tonight. It was of you and Ash and your Crew. You were in the truck. Ash was smiling. Juno and Remi, too. You all were. I grew up with those girls. They're special." Vyr turned and pulled an envelope out of his back pocket. He strode forward and offered it to Grim. "You are doing better than you think. Merry Christmas, Grim."

Vyr gave him a crooked grin and disappeared into the snowstorm.

Grim watched him go before opening the envelope. He pulled out the Crew's paychecks. He wasn't firing them after all. Didn't matter that his dragon didn't like Grim. The man in Vyr was still letting Grim run his mountains.

Grim hadn't said it out loud, but he felt the same way about Vyr. As an Alpha, as a shifter who had to manage a monster inside of him, Grim respected Vyr, too.

Baffled, he turned his frown to where the Red Dragon had disappeared in the snow. "Merry Christmas to you too, Vyr."

NINE

"I think we're supposed to find a Christmas tree *before* Christmas morning," Grim called out as he circled his four-wheeler around the front of 1010. He'd tied a huge plastic sled behind it.

"Dibs on the back of the sled," Juno said, sprinting for it.

"Why would you want the back?" Remi asked, crunching through the snow toward the sled. "Grim will go too fast so there is a million percent chance of you falling off."

"Better than getting showered with snow for the next mile," Juno said, holding on to the edges like Grim would take off at any moment.

Grim said, "If it takes a mile to find a Christmas

tree, I'm leaving these mountains and never coming back. I told you all eight times there is a perfectly good one right there." He pointed to the closest pine tree to the trailer park.

Ash scrunched up her face as she made her way to the ATV. "But then it wouldn't be a Christmas adventure. It would just be you chopping down a tree with an ax, just like every other day. At least this way you can dump Juno off the back."

Grim huffed a laugh and stood up straight on the four-wheeler while she climbed up behind him.

"Ash, what are you doing?" Juno asked. "There is room on the sled!"

"I love you both, but I would rather snuggle Grim than you."

"Traitor," Remi accused through a big ol' grin.

Rhett and Kamp came barreling through the trees on their ATV's, zigzagging so carelessly, they almost crashed into each other twice. Both were laughing like lunatics.

Christmas morning had been fun and simple. Breakfast together and no presents because they hadn't gotten paid until the banks were already closed. But Ash liked it this way. Today was all about spending time together, and she had a feeling today was going to be her new favorite day.

Rhett gunned his quad and then hit the brakes, spinning the back end and spraying Grim and Ash with snow as he came to a jerky stop. "What does Rebble think about that?"

Grim was growling a feral sound. "He called you a hero and is laughing. Now guess what the Reaper says about it?"

Rhett gave Grim an oh-shit look, hit the gas and sped away.

"And that's why he's last in the Crew," Kamp said proudly, like being Fifth was a big accomplishment.

Ash laughed a lot in Rogue Pride. Everyone was funny and didn't take life too seriously.

Grim and Kamp took off after Rhett, and behind her, the girls were cracking up as they held onto the sled, shifting their body weight back and forth to try to stay on. They were all the way to the parking area down the mountain by the time they caught up to Rhett. As Grim slowed, a rumbling noise sounded just over the engine.

It was a car headed this way. Grim tensed under Ash's arms. "You hear that?" he asked.

"Yes," Ash whispered. "Is it Vyr?"

Grim cut the engine of the ATV and dismounted. He stood sentry in front of them, and Kamp and Rhett joined him.

Sixty-three seconds later, a car climbed the last snowy hill and broke through the trees. "It's Sophia," Kamp murmured, stepping forward and waving. "And Raider!"

A little boy was waving frantically out the back window as Kamp's ex parked the car. She stepped out first with a grin. "Merry Christmas!" she called to them. Whoa, she was beautiful, with chocolate brown skin, tight, dark curls with blond tips and a gorgeous smile. Remi struggled to her feet off the sled and bounded over to her. She gave her a big hug as Kamp opened the cub's door.

This was the first time Ash had ever seen Raider. He was a shade between his father's fair skin and his mother's dark skin, with the same blond-streaked curls as Sophia. Sturdy little cub. He was four or maybe five, but built like a little tank already. And when he jumped up into Kamp's arms from the back seat, he was growling loudly. Oh, he had a little brawler lion cub inside him.

"I figured you could use a half day with Raider," Sofia explained breathlessly. "We opened presents at the crack of dawn, and then he asked if he could see you and the Crew today and Change in the snowy mountains, so here we are."

"Where's your mate? You could've both spent the day out here," Kamp said.

"Back at the new house cooking a huge feast for me and a bunch of our friends. It's our new time hosting at the new place. He couldn't leave the turkey alone for this long so I told him I would head straight back. Would you mind dropping him off tonight?" she asked Kamp.

"Crap no, I don't mind." He ruffled Raider's head. "And you don't say crap."

Raider giggled. "Can I see Waffles?"

"Yes, but how about you help us cut down a Christmas tree first?"

"Yes! I'm really good at chopping." Raider flattened out his hand and made hacking motions against Kamp's shoulder, which caused Kamp to twitch around like he was being chopped up. More giggles from Raider, and Ash was smitten. They were putting good magic into these mountains. All this echoing laughter was making the forest happy.

Sophia said her hellos and goodbyes and then headed back down the mountains just as another car came up the snowy road.

The lady driving it brought instant tears to Ash's eyes.

The rest of her 10:10 wish had come true.

"Grandma?" Grim said on a frozen breath. He looked so stunned, staring at the rental car parking in front of him.

Rose got out with tears rimming her eyes and a quivering smile. "Hi, Grim."

Ash squeezed his hand as he led her over to the only steady family he'd ever had before this Crew. He hesitated for a moment before he pulled Grandma Rose in for a bear hug. The Reaper wasn't even growling right now.

Grim was happy. Ash could tell because she could feel it coming off him. That was a lot of joy if the body couldn't even contain it and, oh, she breathed for Grim's joy. He deserved the world after everything he'd been through.

"What are you doing here?" he asked, still hugging the small, silver-haired woman.

"I got a call from a man yesterday morning who told me he'd booked me a plane ticket to be here with my grandson for his first real Christmas."

"Who?" Grim asked. "Who called you?"

"Oh, I think you know."

Ash sure did. She would bet her wardrobe that Vyr had done this after hearing her wish the other night in the bar. Grim didn't trust him, and he was right to be careful. Vyr was making strange decisions. But Ash had known him from childhood, and that wily dragon also had good in him. Like his father before him.

Vyr had done a kind thing and given Grim his grandma for the first Christmas outside of the Tarian Pride. His first Christmas as just himself, multi-monstered man, mate of Ash, Alpha of the Rogue Pride Crew. He wasn't the enforcer for the Pride anymore. He wasn't their killer. He wasn't just the Reaper. Or the good lion. Or the man. He was everything. Anything he wanted to be, he would be. Ash would make sure of it.

Oh, it would be a long road for him to get where he wanted to get, but she would be there every step of the way. And so would Rose. So would Rogue

Pride.

Grim wasn't alone. Not anymore and never again.

As if he could feel the pride and emotion roiling through her, he pulled her in close and hugged her and his grandma up tight before releasing them.

"Rhett," Grim said. "Get on the sled. Grandma is taking your ATV."

"I call dibs on the spot right behind Juno," he said, waggling his eyebrows as he jogged toward the sled.

It was chaos and pandemonium, everyone loading up and rearranging seats. Raider was climbing up in front of Kamp on his ATV, and Ash's very best friends were piling on the sled in front of Rhett. Rose turned her quad on like a pro, and when Ash turned around, Grim was standing by theirs, his hand offered to help her on.

And he was still wearing her favorite smile.

Sometimes a good man could get caught in a bad cycle, but if he had the right people to prop him up when he was learning to stand again, he could become greater than anyone could ever imagine.

That was Grim. Her good man. Her mate whom, as of yesterday, was officially registered as hers. Her Alpha. Her bridge to this beautiful life.

This Christmas was very special because it was a marker for Grim's improvement. A year from today, they would be doing this tradition, hunting the perfect tree, and Grim would have a moment like this, where he was looking at Ash with such deep emotion in his yellow eyes. And she would think back on the year and have such pride in how far he'd come. She knew it would be that way. His quality of life had turned around already because he'd accepted his throne here and let the people he cared about the most...*in*. No more being stuck on the outside for Grim.

This Christmas was special because Rogue Pride was all together, a complete Crew, building bonds that would last their entire lives.

Ash slid her hand into Grim's and let him help her up. She sat behind him and wrapped her arms around his middle. He lifted her hand to his lips, kissed the base of her wrist, and then pressed her palm inside his open jacket against his steady heartbeat. "That'll always be yours," he murmured.

And she understood.

She, Ashlynn Kane, the girl who used to be confused by everything...understood.

Grim had given her his heart to keep safe for always.

As long as she lived, she would never forget this feeling of utter certainty, knowing this was just the beginning of their great big story.

This Christmas was special because it was the first of many to come.

New Vyr

(Daughters of Beasts, Book 5)

T S JOYCE

NEW Vyr

A SONS OF BEASTS SHORT STORY

ONE

This wasn't how Vyr Daye's happily ever after was supposed to be.

He pushed open the door of the mansion but could tell Riyah wasn't here. The creaking of the door echoed, and the place was dark and cold.

Inside of him, the Red Dragon moved in discomfort. It wasn't because this place was dark like the shifter prison he'd almost died in. It wasn't because of the cold that made the dragon slower and weaker. It wasn't because he wasn't greeted by his Sons of Beasts Crew. Again.

It was because he still couldn't push into Riyah's mind. She'd kicked him out of her head months ago and hadn't lifted the veil for him to feel what she was feeling. Not even once. Not even when she slept.

That distance made his dragon want to burn everything.

Being an Alpha was supposed to be so different.

Being open about his dragon with the public was supposed to be different.

Happily ever after was supposed to be different.

Vyr had ruined everything.

The worst part? He was always going to ruin everything. Monsters had destinies just like everyone else, and sometimes good people got caught up in the fate of demons. And sometimes it broke them.

Vyr set his duffle bag on the scuffed wood floors and flipped on the light.

Nox was sitting there. Vyr startled hard, but kept his face blank. He was getting better at showing no emotion. Just like his father, the Blue Dragon, Damon Daye.

"I can't sense you anymore," Vyr murmured, frowning. Maybe it was another hallucination. Those happened more frequently now. "What have you done?"

"Not me, Sky-Lizard. Riyah's protecting us now." He pointed to his head. "No trespassing in the old noggin' anymore. Not after that war with Rogue Pride."

"It wasn't a war with them," Vyr growled, feeling utterly betrayed. By Nox. By Riyah. Fuck. Softer, he said, "I was only after the Tarian Pride."

Nox snarled up his lip, and his eyes flashed bright blue for a moment. And then he forced a smile and a laugh while shoving a present across the coffee table. It was in the shape of a book and wrapped in paper with tacos and Santa hats. "I got you a belated Christmas present."

"The assload of coal you dumped on the front lawn wasn't sufficient?" Vyr asked.

"Just so you don't get joy out of opening your thoughtful gift," Nox said, standing and stretching his back. "I got you a book called How Not To Be A Possessive Dick For Dummies."

"That's the most offensive gift I've ever been given," Vyr said, allowing a small internal smile but nothing more.

"Thank you."

"Wasn't a compliment."

Nox shrugged up his shoulder and made his way toward the hallway. "Hey, Vyr?" he asked, turning just before he disappeared.

Vyr dragged his gaze from the present. "Yes?"

"You know who still believes in you?"

Vyr couldn't name anyone, so he answered with a head shake.

Nox thumped himself on the chest and gritted his teeth. "Me. Nevada. Candace. Torren will never quit, even if you succeed in burning the whole fuckin' world." Nox swallowed hard and gritted out, "And Riyah. She's still here, man."

"Protecting my own Crew from me."

"So stop giving her a reason to protect us. This is the way it was always going to be—"

"No, this isn't okay—"

"It is! You know why? Because you're the real End of Days, right? It was never Kane who was going to claim the world. It was always you. Guess who called that shit from birth? Me! And Torren! And we picked you anyway because we believe in you. It was always going to be up and down. Good, steady times punctuated by rock-fuckin'-bottom and your control slipping. But you know what you learn when you're at the top? Nothing. And you know what you learn at rock bottom?" Nox snarled up his lip and his eyes flashed brighter. "Everything."

Vyr's eyes burned, but he didn't know why. He'd cried twice in his whole life. Once the day he thought the New IESA had killed his dragon. And once on the worst day of his life, six months ago. What was wrong with him? He only knew one thing for sure. "I've failed her—"

"Shut the fuck up. None of that self-pity shit here, Red Dragon. Riyah knew what she was getting when she chose you. And so did the rest of us. Remember that video you made us? When you needed us in that prison? When you needed us to be there for you? You said, 'Come. Here.' And we did. No questions asked, we came for you." Nox jammed a finger at Vyr. "You owe us. Come. Here." He swallowed hard, his eyes rimmed with moisture that fell to his cheeks, and he ran his hand down his face roughly to dry it. "Come back."

Nox disappeared into the dark hallway. He'd changed over this last trip. He was angry now. Not normal Nox who was angry at the world but kept his sense of humor. This was a tired Nox. This was a side of him Vyr had never seen. Vyr's fault. This was all on him.

He needed to figure out a way to stop the Red Dragon from his plans and fix his Crew.

In a hoarse voice, Vyr called out, "Where is she?"

"Orchard," was all the Son of the Cursed Bear said.

Vyr rolled his eyes closed and sighed. Fuck.

TWO

He was here. Vyr. Not *her* Vyr, because Riyah hadn't seen hide nor hair of *her* Vyr in months. But the shell was here.

She fought the temptation to let her walls down, but she couldn't let him feel the sadness she did right now. Not when she was looking at the tiny gravestones on the ground, in the very back corner of her very favorite place—her orchard.

She knew it wasn't the real him, and he would be like he always was—distant. But she still got excited to see him anyway, because she loved him unconditionally. She loved him to the stars and back, and her heart would feel that way until her last breath. He was everything.

She pushed off her knees and smiled at the stones because that's where she was at. This was the point in her healing she had reached. She could smile again, and it was a big deal.

Power pulsed inside of her, but she gritted her teeth and closed her eyes, focused on keeping the energy inside of her. This place was sacred, and it deserved better than her losing control and decimating it.

Everyone thought Vyr was the danger. And he was. But he wasn't the only one.

It was the day after Christmas, and the snow was thick and crisp on the ground. She should've been cold, but she didn't feel much anymore. The rows of fruit trees had lost all their leaves that autumn, and this place looked barren and cold to anyone else. But to her, this was home. Why? Because Vyr had made it for her. He'd bought this land, planted the trees, and built the giant shed for all the equipment. For the last two years, he'd helped her harvest the fruit and sell them at flea markets like she'd done with her mother as a child.

Riyah was a witch, natural born, just like her mother was. Like Vyr was and his mother, Clara Daye.

She could feel him getting closer. Vyr, Vyr, Vyr. She began to jog. His mind was open.

Where are you? Riyah, where are you?

She wanted to answer him, but she couldn't lift the veil. Her feelings would set off his volatile dragon.

She ran faster. There he was. She could see his aura long before she could make out his facial features. Muddy brown. No more purple. He hadn't been a pretty color in months. No, he wasn't her Vyr, but at least part of him was here.

Long, powerful strides headed straight for her. She wasn't imagining him, not this time. He was here. He was home. She pushed her legs faster. His red hair was mussed. Longer on top, short on the sides. He'd gotten a haircut somewhere while he was away. Bright silver eyes with elongated pupils. The Red Dragon. He was bigger than when he'd left. He'd put on seven...maybe ten pounds of muscle. It was obvious in his tight white sweater. His powerful legs were pushing against the fabric of his jeans as he moved faster toward her. His skin was so pale. It was as white as the snow he walked on. And the closer she got, the more exhausted his eyes looked.

Instinct told her to stop. Experience told her to

stop. He would reject her again. Dozens of little rejections, but she wanted him to let her in. And maybe, just maybe, it would be different this time.

She didn't stop. She ran right into his outstretched arms and held on as tight as she could. She didn't cry. Riyah didn't do that anymore. Her tears had dried up a long time ago. But her heart was breaking in a good way. He was actually hugging her. Holding her.

And then he placed his lips right near her ear and whispered, "Why did you bury them here?"

Riyah looked up at the sky and held him tight. He should hear this. He should talk about it. "Because you made this place for me. And they deserve your love, too."

"Fuck," he choked out. His hands gripped her jacket, and he pulled her body so hard against him that it was hard to breathe. But it felt so good.

"I miss you," she murmured brokenly.

"I'm here."

"That's not what I meant," she said, easing back. She cupped the red beard that dusted his jaw and searched those dragon eyes. "I miss *you*."

He held her gaze for a moment, and then she

witnessed it—the shutdown. He made a clicking sound behind his teeth and looked off into the woods with that vacant stare she'd come to know so well.

Anger boiled through her blood, and a little piece of her wanted to slap him just to remind him she was still here. "I exist, you know? I'm the one waiting at home while you claim new territory."

"You could come with me."

"I don't support you giving in to the dragon. You're addicted, Vyr. With every territory you allow your dragon to claim, you have less control over him."

"I never had control of him," he said blandly.

Her fury got the best of her as she stomped past him. She lifted the veil just enough to put one word in his head. *Liar.*

Vyr yelled, and she heard the sound of him falling to his knees behind her. When she turned, he was hunched over, clutching his head. "Riyah," he whispered. "What have you been hiding from me?"

She lifted her chin. "I'll show you when you're strong enough."

"You'll taunt me with a glimpse of it?"

"Taunt you? You think I want to do this alone? I love you, Vyr. I love you!" A wave of power blasted out from her with the last word, and the snow blew away in a perfect circle around them. They were left in the center of a frozen field.

"How? If I keep...keep..."

"It's my loss, too, Vyr. I lost them, too! I lost..." She strode over to him, sank down onto his lap, and hugged his shoulders tight, daring him to try to escape her this time. "I lost them, but even worse, I lost you at the same time. You've made me go through this alone."

"You have Candace and Nevada."

"I need you."

"Torren and Nox are understanding."

"They aren't my mates, Vyr! They're my Crew!"

"I don't know how to do this!" Vyr yelled, hugging her so tight her ribs cracked. "I can't fix it. I can't protect you."

"Is that what this is about? Protecting me? From pain? You're making it worse by not being here for me."

"Give me any person who would ever hurt you, and I would turn them to ash and devour them without blinking. I always knew my role. I was supposed to keep you safe, Riyah. And I was the one who poisoned you instead."

"Poisoned me?" she asked softly. "Vyr, you can't believe that. For a while, I was their mother." *Oh, God, give me strength to just tell him how it is.* "My two perfect boys."

"Perfect. They were gargoyles."

"Don't call them that," she snapped. "They were perfect. Who could've stopped them from shifting before they were ready? Who could've stopped their little dragons? Hmm? Had they lived, they would be just like you," she said, her voice dipping to a proud whisper. "And I would've loved every second."

"They were born with wings, Riyah. They will always be born like that. Beaston said it's the way the world has to balance us. We're each too big. There's too much power between us. Offspring—"

"Don't call them that."

A long rumble emanated from him. "Our *children* would end the world. But you're my mate, and to me, you are the world. You want to be a mother, and you deserve to be a mother. I want to see you holding my child, and I can't give that to you. This is the consequence of our power. You settled in so many ways the day you chose me."

"Vyr," she murmured, running her hands through his hair. She smiled. "You still don't see what I see, you silly man."

"What do you see?" Heartache tainted his voice.

She pressed her hand against his pounding heart. "To me, you're also the whole world. You think I don't have those moments, too? The ones where I feel like I failed? The ones where I'm sad and I miss them and I feel like I let you down for not making you a dad?" She shrugged. "I know I can't ever give you that either. But you won't fix it by feeding your dragon power. You will ruin us and this Crew. And probably the whole damn world by the time the Red Dragon is done."

Vyr traced her lips with his fingertip. "You smiled. I haven't seen that in a long time."

"You gave me that smile."

"I have an admission," he rumbled, brushing her dark hair from her face.

"Tell me everything." She always said that when he had admissions. "I'll keep your secrets safe. Always."

He inhaled deeply. "When I'm gone, hunting new territories...I have a dream. Just one, over and over, every night I'm away from you."

Riyah wrapped her legs around him. This was the most he'd spoken to her in months. "Is it a dirty dream?"

Vyr snorted. "No. I dream we're on our bed, and I'm tracing your freckles." He lifted his finger from just below her lips to her cheek and began to trace the dark spots she'd inherited from her mother. "And you're looking at me with this little smile."

She sighed and leaned into his touch.

"Yeah," he said, staring at her lips. "A smile just like that one. And then your freckles move and change, then suddenly we're on our backs on the floor of that prison, looking up at those stars you put on the ceiling. But the words don't say 'I'm yours' anymore. They say 'I'm theirs.' When I wake up, my whole chest is on fire, and I wish it could be true. That you could be theirs. If you were with someone normal, you could have a baby."

"A witch baby."

"Be serious."

"I am being serious. My genetics aren't exactly cream of the crop either, Vyr. Which is why I've come to a decision."

Vyr frowned. "What decision?"

"I don't want to try again."

"For another baby?"

"I went to see Beaston." She nearly choked on the admission and repeated it softer. "I went to see Beaston. And when I asked if I would ever be a mother, I pushed my way into his head. Oh, he knew what I was doing. He gave me this wicked smile and stopped talking out loud. I could see what he saw for me. I'd wanted answers, and he gave them to me. Thoroughly. If our children were to survive, no one else would. It would be the coming of the end, and no one could stop it. I saw in his head, Vyr. I was holding a little blond-haired baby on my hip. He had glowing green eyes, like his animal was already awake and watching. You were standing next to me, and all around us was fire. I don't know whether that was a yes or a no on me being a mother. But I haven't been able to think about anything else. I feel empty since I lost the twins. Like my tummy has a hole in it, and it's so big that it ate up my heart, too." She shrugged up one shoulder. "But maybe we are only meant to be really good to Torren's son. You know? Maybe that's our role. Maybe I can be good with being the best aunt to the new little Kong. Dane is so cute. And I still get to watch you be the best uncle to him. And to Nox and Nevada's kids when the time comes. Between little Kongs and Noxes, we'll have our hands full in this Crew," she said optimistically.

Vyr's frown wrinkled his whole forehead. "This is a big change. Are you sure you're okay with this?"

Yes, she said into his mind and let him feel what she was feeling for just a moment. Acceptance.

Vyr rolled his eyes closed and his head back. "God, I've missed the feel of you."

She grabbed her boobs and said earnestly, "I've missed the feel of you, too."

He chuckled. Chuckled!

"I've missed that sound," she said in a rush.

The smile faded from his lips. "I don't know how to get back to the way I was," he murmured.

"Maybe you aren't meant to be the man you were. Maybe you are meant for something bigger. Growth isn't an easy thing, Vyr. If it was, everyone would do it. You will have big phases of growth over and over, like a snake shedding his skin, until you can become strong enough to control the Red Dragon."

"You have so much more faith in me than I

deserve."

"No. I just know what you're capable of. No man could protect the world from the Red Dragon but you. No one else is strong enough. But you've done it all these years." Riyah swallowed audibly. "Stay."

"I can't," he whispered, dragging her palm to his lips.

Riyah tugged the beard that hung from his chin and shook his face gently. "Stay."

Vyr dropped his gaze and shook his head slightly.

"Okay. You're telling me you aren't there yet. Aren't strong enough to stop this yet. But I'm through the worst of the mourning—at least I hope to God I am—and now it's time to focus on you, not our loss. And not my pain. Oh, I know you blame yourself. It's not a coincidence you started claiming new mountains right when I lost the babies. I just wasn't strong enough to travel and watch you spiral, too. In a way, we both had to cope on our own. That part surprised me, but everyone is different, and the both of us flinched inward and absorbed the blows. Apart. You pushed me away, and I got quiet and I waited and waited, but I'm tired of doing that now, Vyr."

"Are you leaving me?" he asked, zero surprise or

emotion in his voice.

"No, ridiculous man. The opposite."

"What do you mean?"

"I'm gonna be by your side while you spiral."

"You support me taking over the Tarian Pride territory now?"

"Fuck no," she scoffed. "I'm gonna bitch at you the whole time, chew loudly when I eat, interrupt your sleep, and make you miserable with my presence in general until you tire of traveling to obsess over those stupid mountains—"

"I'm in!" Nox's voice echoed through the orchard.

Riyah and Vyr looked around, but he was nowhere to be found.

"I'm also in!" Torren, the giant silverback shifter and best friend of Vyr yelled from somewhere equally mysterious.

"Oh, we're also in!" That was Nevada's voice.

"Are babies allowed?" Candace called.

"Oh...my God," Vyr griped. "Have you all been here listening the entire time?"

"Yeah," Nox called. "We brought popcorn."

Riyah scrunched up her face and slid her hands over Vyr's shoulders. "What if we'd had loud welcome-home sex?"

"That's what we brought the popcorn f— Ow!" Nox exclaimed as the sound of a slap hitting skin echoed through the orchard. If Riyah had to guess, Candace was the one who'd whacked him.

Riyah giggled. How long had it been since she'd made that sound? God, it was good to have Vyr—she studied his muddy brown aura—or at least part of Vyr home.

"There's something that bothers me about Beaston's vision," Vyr said as he rocked upward and settled her on her feet.

"What?"

"You said the baby had glowing green eyes."

"So?"

"So you're a new-ish shifter and maybe don't know how the genetics work on this stuff. A child would have either your eyes or mine, and neither of us have green eyes." He looked utterly disturbed.

"Okay, well what do you think that means?"

Vyr was looking at her in the strangest way, his silver eyes roiling with some emotion she couldn't understand. She reached for his mind, but he'd shut her out.

"Vyr, what?"

"I won't be the child's father."

Riyah's heart pounded against her breast bone. "What?"

"If you become a mother, it won't be with me. Either something happens to me or…"

"Or what?"

Vyr sighed a frozen breath. "Or you do what you should've done a long time ago."

Baffled, she shook her head. "I don't understand."

"You leave me and find someone who can give you a better life."

Riyah stood on her tippy-toes and kissed him hard. It was the kind of kiss that was a little like a middle finger. It was teeth hitting his and a bite it the middle that she hoped hurt him. She wrapped her fingers around his throat and squeezed, letting her power pulse gently from her palm. After she pulled her lips from his, she whispered, "Don't you ever talk like that again. I don't care what the vision was. I won't leave you. Not ever."

"Why not?"

"Because I'm the Red Dragon's treasure." She shoved him in the shoulder hard and then slipped her hand into his. "And you're mine, too."

THREE

The green-eyed child haunted him. Vyr lay beside Riyah, studying the curve of her cheek as she slept. Six months ago, he'd done this every morning, except it was the swell of her belly he'd been memorizing. He'd had such dreams for his sons. His dragon... Fuck. Vyr flinched at the pounding headache that was forming behind his eyes. He would have to Change soon. He'd been desperate to control the Changes because the dragon grew more powerful with each shift. He couldn't keep him from burning anymore. He knew he couldn't. He could see the Red Dragon's plans so clearly in his head.

Four mountain ranges in six months. Vyr had tried to compromise. Each territory he claimed, he found the broken ones, the shifters with nowhere to go but slamming against that rock bottom Nox had spoken of. And then he gave the mountains he claimed to them. He'd found the damned, the damaged, and he'd given them homes. Because that was the legacy he hoped some would remember when he lost control of the dragon completely. He hoped they remembered the man who tried to save as many as possible.

The dragon wanted offspring, and the man wanted to see Riyah happy, cooing to a child he had given her, crying happy tears like she had done sometimes before everything went wrong. After that awful day...

Well, she only cried sad tears now.

Beautiful mate. Her freckles were dark against her pale skin, and her brunette hair was all curled up, fanning across her pillow. That pillow would smell like her shampoo when she got up. He always sniffed it after she stumbled into the bathroom to take a shower in the mornings. He missed the smell of her pillow when he was out re-burning his territories or hunting new ones.

But for now, he was here, and she was sleeping

soundly, her hand resting on his hip like she'd put it there in the middle of the night just to make sure he stayed with her. She still felt safe around him, he could tell. God, had any living creature during the planet's entire existence ever loved another as much as he loved Riyah? He couldn't imagine it. She really was the treasure of the Red Dragon, but so *so* much more. Before Riyah, his chest had been empty, but from the day he'd met her, she'd started building a heart in there. And then she'd crawled inside and made a home and made sure his heart kept working.

She was his treasure, but she was also the heart of the dragon.

His attention flickered out the window. There wasn't movement that had drawn his gaze there; it was just the sky. *Come fly. Touch the clouds. Burn everything,* it encouraged him. *Fill me with smoke.*

The dragon roiled inside of him, searing through his veins like acid. Vyr didn't even wince. His whole life was pain. At some point, he'd just gotten used to it.

There was one strand of hair on Riyah's cheek, and soft as a feather, he pushed it back with the tip of his finger. As his touch slid across her skin, the corner of her mouth curved into a slow smile, but faded when he lifted his finger away.

So beautiful. He cupped her cheek, sure to make his touch as soft as a breeze. The tiny smile returned.

His heart.

Burn everything.

Vyr closed his eyes against the dawn light and just disappeared into how soft her skin was. The distance between them had lifted, but that was all Riyah's doing. She made him feel...forgiven.

"You are forgiven," she whispered.

When he opened his eyes, her bright blue polar bear eyes were locked on his. The smile still lingered.

"You are forgiven for everything you have done, and everything you will do."

"How can you?"

"Because I love you."

The heart she'd built felt like it was shattering. His body broke apart a lot lately.

"You're worried about the child," she said. "You've been thinking so loud."

He reached for her with his mind, but it felt like nothing was there...like Riyah was a ghost. Was she a ghost?

"I'm still here."

He dragged her closer and hugged her tight against his chest. Soft curves and skin on skin. He loved that she slept naked with him. "I don't want you to choose someone else," he murmured against her hair right before he kissed it.

"Vyr, I wish you could see yourself from my eyes. You don't have to worry about me leaving. Not ever."

She slid her knee over his hip, pressed against his erection. He was always hard for her in the mornings, always riled up, always turned on. She was so soft. Vyr slid his hand to her ass and squeezed it hard, drawing her right against him as he rolled his hips.

She let off this sound that drove him crazy. Rolling his hips harder, he kissed her. Riyah's hands eased down his chest, drawing heat where her body met his. God, she consumed him. Desperate, Vyr cupped between her legs and pushed a finger into her, making sure she was ready to take him. So wet already. Good mate. He rolled her over, spread her knees apart, and slid into her, his entire body flexing with the motion. Deeper and deeper, he pushed until he was buried all the way inside of her tight pussy. Vyr held her hands above her head and thrust into her again and again, shallow because he knew the buttons to push on his mate. She liked it hard and quick.

His whispered name on her lips made him even harder, and his control began to slip. "Come for me, Riyah," he rumbled against her ear, gripping her wrists tighter as he moved inside of her. Deep. Deep. Quick. Fuck, he was almost there, stroking into the tight, wet space she'd given to him. He was bucking into her now like some rutting animal. "Riyah, I can't stop. You feel so fucking good I can't stop. Aaaaaaaah," he groaned as the pressure in his dick released, spewing his seed into her in throbbing bursts.

Riyah cried out and arched against the mattress, fists clenched, eyes rolled back into her head, hair wild, body...his. Her tight little pussy gripped his pulsing cock so hard as they came together. He took care of her, drew out every last clench of ecstasy from her body, moving inside her until she was completely sated. He released her hands and cupped the back of her neck, kissed her gently, so she knew how much he loved her. She liked when he was sweet after he made her come. And then against her lips, he uttered the words he knew would ruin it all. "I have to leave again soon."

Her body tensed, so he waited until she relaxed again before he continued. "I need to re-burn Grim's Mountains. Or claim new territory. Or...something."

Riyah rolled him to the side and hugged him up tight, leaving him buried inside of her. "Wow," she murmured after a few seconds.

"Hmm?"

"That's the first time I've ever heard you call them Grim's Mountains."

Vyr frowned at the window, frowned at the gray sky outside. Huh.

"What is it about Grim?" she murmured. "Of all the Crew's you've helped, of all the Alpha's, you can't seem to stay away from him. You watch him, don't you?"

The dragon rumbled. She was getting too close. Getting too warm. Smart and clever mate.

He stroked her back, up and down her spine.

"Silence is sometimes an answer, but not with me. I'll keep asking. I'm ready to keep asking now."

Riyah was changing. She was getting stronger. She was pushing more. Beautiful mate. She would need to be strong if anything ever happened to him. If the green-eyed child came to be.

"He's the only shifter I've met who is kind of like me."

"Hey, I'm like you," she groused, pinching his side.

He chuckled and dragged her prodding fingers to his lips, then rested them against his chest between them. "Your polar bear is manageable. She's logical. She's a murder machine, sure, but you control her. You've had control since you were Turned. Grim...he has two lions, and one is like your polar bear, manageable, and one is like the Red Dragon. Unmanageable." *Burn everything.* "Sometimes," he whispered, "I want to kill Grim. He stopped me from claiming the Tarian Pride Mountains. He brought the Daughters of Beasts, and he stopped me. I want to devour his ashes when I'm the dragon, but when I'm me...when I'm the man...I wish we lived in a different world where we could be friends. Where I could ask him how he does it."

"How he does what?" she asked, tracing a heart shape over his left pec.

"How he keeps going. How he keeps trying. We're both absolute shit at being Alphas. Both have been thrust onto thrones we don't deserve by Crews just trying to keep us steady. But I see him trying. I see improvement. And what have I done? I've broken the Sons of Beasts."

"No," she murmured. "You suffered something hard, and your dragon tries to protect you by focusing on anything else. He's not a monster, Vyr. He never was. He's just trying to help in his own way."

Vyr huffed a humorless laugh as the dragon whispered *burn everything* again in his mind. "Some help he is."

"But you haven't burned everything," she said lightly, lifting his arm in a flexing position. "Strong mate."

Vyr leaned in and kissed her. It was a tender one, just like she deserved for being so understanding, one where he sucked on her bottom lip until she let him inside to taste her. She lifted the veil for just a second, and it was enough. She let him have a happy memory, the one where she'd invited all of Damon's Mountains to the orchard he'd planted for her. The one where she'd brought everyone from his past to show them how much he was cared for. Him. An outsider all his life, but his mate had made sure he knew everything was different than he thought. That it was better. Her joy sizzled and snapped through his brain for that second, and he smiled against her lips. There was a tiny aftertaste of pain in the instant she shut down the veil of her mind again, but for that one second, he'd felt okay. God, he'd missed this. Missed her.

He eased away and rumbled, "I want you to come with me."

"To do what?"

"To burn the land."

Sadness washed over her face before she forced a smile. "The last time you asked us to come with you to burn territory, you put our Crew at war with the Tarian Pride and Grim's Crew. You surprised us with that one."

"Is that why you're protecting their minds?" he asked.

Riyah lifted her chin higher and looked him dead in the eyes when she said, "Yes. No more surprise wars. No more Alpha orders until..."

"Finish it."

"Until you can be trusted again."

A knife. Those words were a knife blade, but he

deserved the cut. "I won't declare war on Grim's Crew."

"How do you know?"

"Because I saw him. I talked to him right before Christmas. I sat in the back of this little bar and watched him and his Crew make wishes on ten-ten. And do you know what he wished for?"

"What?"

"To be a better Alpha."

Riyah brushed her fingertips down his beard. "Maybe he really *is* like you."

"He will run my mountains in Oregon until he draws his final breath, and I won't be the one to take that final breath from him. I want at least one of us to be a success story."

"You both will be."

"Riyah—"

"You will be." She'd said it with such conviction echoing through her words that his dragon stilled inside of him.

Burn everything but her.

"I'm ready," she murmured softly.

"Ready for what?"

"To leave them. To leave the orchard." A wicked

little smile took her full lips. "Let's go light some shit on fire." She snapped her fingers and held our palm out, creating a tiny blue flame that flickered just above her skin. But then she closed her fist over the little fire and snuffed it out. Her face turned serious. "In a controlled environment. Where we won't get in trouble or arrested. Where I can give the local law enforcement and fire departments a heads up. And maybe Kane and your father and the other dragons just in case you go nutso. And you can't claim new territory. Just an old one."

Vyr chuckled. She really did have faith in his control over the dragon. "So many rules, Witch."

"Yeah, well, you've been on a burning spree. Someone needs to be the responsible one. I don't want to have to break you out of shifter prison again."

FOUR

It was the ass-crack of dawn, and Riyah was standing in the doorway of the Crew mansion, arms crossed, frowning at Nox, who was out in the front yard scooping the two tons of coal he'd dumped there on Christmas Eve for Vyr's present. He was sitting in the excavator, working the giant metal arm while he held Mr. Diddles, the pet swan, and singing "I got ninety-nine problems and a bitch ain't one," at the top of his lungs. It was the dead of winter and snowing, but he wasn't wearing a shirt. And he wasn't even moving the coal off the lawn. He was just moving it from one pile to a pile closer to the house.

Riyah sighed. He really was a nuisance.

"Nox!" she yelled over the sound of the rumbling

engine. He must've heard her because he looked over at her and started singing louder.

An arrow sailed through the air and banked off the top of the machine with a *piiiiing* sound. Nox ducked, cut the engine, and shouted, "Hey, asshole, you could've hit Mr. Diddles!"

Torren, silverback shifter and guardian of the Red Dragon yelled, "The first lady wants to talk to you. Shut it down!"

Riyah pushed off the doorway she leaned on and walked far enough into the yard to look up to see Torren and Vyr sitting on top of the roof together. Torren was all mussed black hair, huge muscles, and tattoos and, goodness gracious, where was his damn shirt, too? He was holding his favorite crossbow with an arrow already loaded and aimed in Nox's general direction. Awesome.

"Aren't you boys cold?" she asked, gesturing to Vyr's puckered nipples and gooseflesh. "Where are your clothes?"

"Nox bet we couldn't last an hour shirtless without bitching about the cold," Torren muttered. "He said first one who gives in is a pussy."

Vyr looked down at her and muttered in a bored

voice, "I think pussies are awesome."

Oh. Fantastic.

"Okay," she said optimistically. "Bright side, you and Torren are finally talking. Which you haven't done since the war with Grim's Crew. Healing is happening!"

"We aren't talking. We're sitting," Torren growled. "I was here minding my business, shooting at Nox, when Vyr-the-Asshole came and sat by me. I was here first, so why should I move?"

"I own this house, so why should I move?" Vyr asked coolly.

"Well, you always abandon your house, so why should *I* move?"

Riyah was looking back and forth at them with a grin. This was probably good, right?

"Well, I'm Alpha, so fuck you. *You* move. This is my favorite sitting place."

"Well, you're a shitty Alpha, so why don't you go sit there on the ground, beneath me, where you belong."

"This is awesome," Nox called from behind the window of the excavator.

Mr. Diddles honked. The swan couldn't fly and

winters were harsh here, so Nox had dressed him in a little green and pink striped turtleneck and a bowtie. Ms. Tittles, their female swan, had flown south for the winter with last year's babies, but she would be back. Swans mated for life.

"Nox," Vyr rumbled, "I told you to move the coal."

Nox grinned like the Cheshire cat and started up the engine again. He took a scoop of coal off one pile and moved it to the pile ten feet closer to the house. He didn't take his eyes off Vyr the whole time. "I am."

With a deep rumble, Vyr poised himself on the edge of the roof to launch himself at the tractor.

"No, no, no, no!" Riyah and Torren both yelled.

A flash of movement caught Riyah's attention. It was perfect timing because little Dane Maximus Taylor was in gorilla form charging straight this way. A little mini-Torren, the toddler silverback shifter had Changed early and was now a little hellion in these mountains. Nevada and Candace came sprinting around the corner of the mansion after him. Dane was coming straight for Riyah, but this was the game. She was part of his family group and the one who played rough with him the most, thanks to the polar bear in her middle. Vyr probably didn't know that, though. He hadn't been paying attention for months.

"Vyr!" Riyah yelled, desperate to distract Vyr. "Get Dane!"

Vyr's narrowed silver dragon eyes dropped from Nox straight to the little baby gorilla running at Riyah as fast as his four little legs could carry him. His sharp canines had just come in, and he showed her. So cute, but that little Kong could pack a punch with his bite.

Vyr jumped off the roof and landed smoothly right in front of the little gorilla. Dane skidded to a stop in the snow, stood on his back two legs, and clumsily drummed his fists against his chest.

"Bite him," Nox demanded. "Dane, Uncky Nox will give you raspberry Dum Dums if you bite the big ugly sky-lizard."

"Nox!" Torren and Candace both yelled.

Vyr hadn't held Dane since Riyah had lost the twins. Memories flashed across her mind of Vyr watching Dane play and eat and sleep, but never ever picking him up like the rest of the Crew. He'd distanced himself from the child after his loss.

She fully expected him to do the same again. "No biting," he said sternly, his hands clasped formally behind his back.

Dane snapped his teeth. Just a little click, probably learned from Nox.

Vyr narrowed his eyes at the child, but Riyah didn't miss it—the slight smile that curved his lips for just a moment and then disappeared. Kneeling down, Vyr got eye level with the little ruffian and brushed a knuckle along Dane's cheek, tempting a bite. Dane stared back at him with wide, shocked brown eyes and then gripped Vyr's finger in his strong little fist.

Riyah was going to lose it. She was going to lose it! Vyr stood suddenly, but Dane held onto that finger until Vyr drew him smoothly against his chest. The hug happened so fast, Riyah would have missed it if she hadn't been paying attention. It was a quick embrace, and then Vyr stooped and settled Dane on all fours. He ghosted Riyah a glance before he turned abruptly and went inside, the screen door slamming so loud behind him, the sound echoed through the mountains.

Little Kong, as the Crew called Dane, watched Vyr until he was gone, his round eyes steady but confused. Riyah squatted down in the snow and patted her fists on her chest with a smile for the little hellion.

Dane didn't feel like playing rough anymore. He walked sideways to her on all fours, eyes going to the screen door three times before he reached her. He climbed up into her arms and wrapped himself around her torso, held on quietly.

"Little brawler," she crooned, stroking her fingers down his furry back. "Beating your chest at a dragon. You're going to grow up tough and strong just like your mom and dad, aren't you?"

She looked up at Torren, but she couldn't read the expression on his face as he stared at the screen door Vyr had disappeared into.

Riyah sighed. "He did better than he's done in a long time. Vyr will come around. He just needs time."

Torren shook his head slowly, his eyes flashing green. "He's getting worse, and you know it."

Being the most affectionate in the Crew, Nevada stood beside Riyah and rested her cheek against her shoulder, and then she said softly, "You don't give up on him, Torren. That's not what we do."

"I'm still here, aren't I?" Torren growled.

"Hey, fuckface, watch your tone with Nevada," Nox snarled, hopping out of the excavator.

"Oh, God, here we go again," Candace muttered.

Yep, it was fight time. Why? Because the boys needed to. They had all been fighters before they were in a Crew, and now they had an Alpha whose bond had been making them all sick for months. As much as Riyah tried to block the bond between the Crew and Vyr, it was still slowly poisoning the boys anyway. The only thing that made them feel better was fighting.

Torren jumped off the roof and landed hard in the snow. He stood to his full height and roared an inhuman sound. His teeth elongated, and the veins in his neck stood out. Nox didn't waste time with warnings—he just Changed into his massive blond grizzly bear.

"Dammit, Nox!" Nevada yelled. "I just got you those jeans!" The jeans in question were now tatters on the snow as the bear came charging for Torren.

Riyah shook her head sadly. This shouldn't be happening. They shouldn't have to bleed each other to stay steady. She couldn't block any more of the bond to Vyr. She felt helpless to help them, helpless to help Vyr, helpless to get them back on track. Little Kong deserved a good Crew to grow up in, and they were all failing.

Torren's monstrous silverback ripped out of him and barreled toward Nox on all fours.

Riyah didn't want to watch. It was always the same. Violent and brutal, like they hated each other. But she knew better. The boys loved each other, which made their fights even worse. Even more disappointing. She carried Dane to Candace, and as she passed the big front picture window, she looked up to find Vyr staring at Nox and Torren's fight, his eyes vacant, his arms crossed across his broad chest. His attention flickered down to Riyah and then held on Dane for a few seconds before he turned and disappeared into the dark room inside.

Until he disappeared...

That was his move now.

Disappearing.

He would fade and fade until he was completely gone. Unless she stopped him.

"When the boys Change back, bring them inside."

"For what?" Candace asked, taking Dane from her arms.

"I'm calling a Crew meeting."

"Okay," Nevada whispered from beside Candace,

her face averted from the fight. She looked a little green around the gills. "But Vyr hasn't called one in months. I don't think he'll want a meeting."

"I don't give a shit about *wants* anymore. I care about *needs*. What we've been doing isn't working." Riyah shrugged. "Time to change it up."

FIVE

"The boys need to apologize." Riyah looked from Torren, who yawned, to Nox's blank face, to Nevada's downturned gaze, to Candace who was holding Dane. And then she braved a glance at Vyr, but he was staring out the window, sitting by himself on the couch, away from the rest of them.

"Apologize for what?" Torren rumbled low.

"To the Daughters of Beasts."

Vyr huffed a breath and shook his head, eyes still on the window to the snow outside.

Riyah lifted her chin and stood from the bar stool she'd been sitting on. "There are so many broken things we need to fix. So many. And starting now, we will tackle the big ones. One of the cracks in our foundation is that war. Vyr, you forced it. You dragged the boys into it, and they had to go against your friends from Damon's Mountains. It's left poison in our bonds. It's left resentment. I can feel it. I know you can feel it, too."

"I can't feel anything because you've closed everything off," Nevada whispered.

Riyah closed her eyes and pulled her power away from her friends. Not just a little either. She let them see what she'd been absorbing. Let them feel it.

Nevada and Torren doubled over. Nox swallowed hard and looked like he would retch. Candace did gag, and Dane started crying. And Vyr...Vyr ran his hands down his red beard with a shaking hand. *A shaking hand.* She'd never seen her mate shake before.

She sighed in relief at not having to bear the burden of their sick bonds for a few seconds. And then she closed her eyes again and imagined coating them all in her power. The green sickly aura redirected into her, and she steeled herself to take it back without flinching.

When she opened her eyes again, Vyr's eyes were bright silver with elongated pupils and locked on her. "Why are you doing this?"

"Because I don't want you to hurt. I love all of you. If I can stop hurt, I always will."

"How do we apologize?" Nevada asked over the sound of Dane's snuffling.

"Vyr needs to move again. His dragon is searching for something. We have to keep him from claiming new territory, but we can't just tie up the Red Dragon in the basement. We all saw what that shifter prison did to him. He wanted to burn the entire earth when he got out. I think we should go to Grim's Mountains and see his Crew. Vyr sees something special in Grim. A kindred spirit maybe. He can re-burn the mountains there and maybe it'll settle the dragon for a little while."

"Decline," Vyr growled. "I didn't kill them. That was apology enough."

"Well, that's the thing, *mate*," Riyah snarled. "You don't have a fuckin' choice anymore. It's on you to save yourself and save us. Keep going like this, and your dragon will drag us all through hell, and I've already seen it. I'm tired of rock bottom."

"We all are," Torren said low, attention on his mate. Whatever passed between Candace and him, Riyah couldn't tell, but after a few seconds, Torren cleared his throat and said, "I'll need a day to get everything situated with the lumber yard."

Candace nodded slightly and smiled at Torren. It was a small one, but a smile nonetheless. "Nevada and I can keep it running so we don't have to close it down while you're gone. Go. Keep Vyr safe."

Torren huffed. "My job was never to keep him safe. It was to keep the world safe from him."

"An impossible task," Nox sang softly. He'd been uncharacteristically quiet. "Do you feel the sickness of the bonds all the time, Riyah?"

She inhaled deeply. "I don't want to talk about—"

"Do you?" Vyr asked sternly.

Riyah tried to smile. "When it gets really bad, I go to the orchard. I don't know what it is about that place, but it makes everything feel better. Maybe it would be good for you to go sometime, too."

Vyr's face smoothed of all emotion in a heartbeat. "I'll make the travel arrangements." He stood and made his way toward the office, his stride stiff and fast, his hands clasped behind his back.

Riyah was good and done with these infinite rejections, though, so she stood and followed him. No more escaping her. No more running away. He was sitting in the office chair by the time she got there, his back to her, the drawer open.

"I love you, you know," she said. "Always will."

He closed the drawer and cracked his knuckles, stared at the dark laptop screen. "I know. I saw that when you lifted the wall. I wish I could just get better for you." A long, low dragon's snarl filled the room, rattling the floor beneath her feet. "Fuck," he whispered, scrubbing his hands over his face until the noise faded.

Riyah approached him slowly, slipped her arms around his shoulders, and kissed the side of his neck gently. "Go see them."

"See who?" he asked carefully.

She reached over him and pulled the desk drawer open. Oh, she'd found his hidden stash months ago. It was a pair of ultrasound pictures, worn at the corners as if he'd held them a hundred times.

"See *them*."

As she pulled away, he suddenly grabbed her wrist and kissed the palm of her hand. "Everything will be okay."

She smiled again. Actually smiled. "I know it will. No one will ever have as much faith in another person as I have in you."

"You're not going to let me fail, are you?" he asked softly.

And with utter confidence, she inhaled deeply and uttered, "No."

She would do horrible things to make sure he succeeded in controlling the dragon. She would use her power against the Red Dragon himself if pushed. Come hell or high water, Vyr was going to cage his demons and gain control again.

Even if she had to be the cage.

SIX

A hundred miles stretched from Vyr to the two little stones at the edge of Riyah's orchard. His legs were frozen, just like every other time he'd tried to do this.

For him, there was no urge for closure. That meant saying goodbye to them, and he didn't want that. He wanted to keep his fantasies and what ifs. What if they had lived? What would they have been like, what would they have looked like? Would they have red hair like his, or dark like Riyah's? Would they be witches, too? Would they inherit his and Riyah's power? He imagined them red-haired with their mother's dark freckles. What color would their dragons have been? Shit. Their dragons had killed them. He shouldn't even think of that half of them. He should hate that part of them. The monsters in them had Changed in Riyah's stomach, and neither twin had made it.

And now Vyr's dragon would kill him.

Riyah was slipping. The veil between them was thin now, and he could see in her mind for a split second at a time when he touched her. When he'd kissed her palm and held it, he'd seen it. A vision of her standing on the ground below his dragon, her hands outstretched, anguish in her eyes, her hair wild in the wind, power pulsing from her fingertips right at him.

It wasn't Torren who would save the world from him. It was Riyah.

Strong mate.

He clenched his hands behind his back as the dragon clawed at his skin. *Just look at the little stones. Say hello to them. Talk to them.*

Vyr gritted his teeth and forced one step and then another. The dragon was revolting inside of him, and every cell in his body was burning, but fuck it. Riyah said she came here when she was sick from pain. Maybe, just maybe, this place could help him heal too.

Why did it still feel like a hundred miles? He could see the stones so clearly, poking out from the new snow. Riyah had buried the twins between two oak trees that had been planted in their honor. She had placed a wooden bench beside them.

The wind kicked up. It wasn't natural, wasn't another cold front blowing in, wasn't a storm on the horizon. It was Vyr. He couldn't control his power sometimes. Not anymore. The more the dragon spiraled, the more his powers grew. Snow parted in a straight line to the little headstones.

Barely audible over the wailing of the wind, he whispered, "I don't want to do this."

****

I don't want to do this.

Riyah gasped and sat straight up in bed. Her body was wracked with chills, and she was drenched in sweat. Was she going to get sick? Everything around her was blurry, so she blinked hard. It smelled like the bedroom, but something was pelting her in the face. Snow?

"Vyr?" she asked to no answer.

Riyah stumbled out of bed, but she couldn't see the floor. Her feet landed in snow, one in front of the other, but when she looked down, they weren't her feet. They were Vyr's thick-soled boots with the scuff on the right toe. In front of her, the snow blasted outward, leaving a trail that lead to the boys.

Vyr? she thought, but he still didn't answer. He was staring straight ahead as he walked through her orchard. What was happening?

She tried to shut the wall between them, but it was stuck. No, not stuck. It was as if his power was prying it open. The air moved around him, like waves of heat on a summer day in the desert. She was burning up. Her skin was hot, and the pain was almost unbearable.

She couldn't see the bedroom, only the orchard. Feeling around the room blindly, her hands found nothing but air. Terrified, she screamed out, "Nox!" She didn't know why he was the one she called and not the girls or Torren. It just tumbled out of her mouth, the name of the least reliable of the Crew.

Three more steps through the parted snow. The drifts had piled up to the side, guiding her in a straight line to them...the boys. Her babies. Three steps, one, two, three, and then hands were on her.

"Shit!" Nox yelped, flinching away. "Riyah, your

skin is burning. Torren!" he yelled.

The waves of heat melted the snow beside her, turning the earth to mud in moments.

I don't want to do this," Vyr whispered again.

"Do what?" Nox asked. "Riyah! Do what?"

Had she spoken Vyr's words? Where was she? In the room still?

"Nox," she whispered raggedly. "Help him."

"Where?" Nox yelled.

"The orchard."

"Shhhhit."

"Let's take my truck." Torren's voice. "She needs to come with us."

"Well, she's fuckin' floating in the air like we need to exorcise a demon and I can't fuckin' touch her. Her skin feels like an oven."

"Hurts," she whispered.

"You break his bedroom window, Vyr's gonna kill you," Torren growled.

The sound of shattering glass was deafening. Nox wasn't the one to spout rules to.

She took three more steps toward the little gravestones, but her body was suddenly hurled to the side. Then there was relief.

She was on her hands and knees in the orchard now, a deep rumble vibrating through her. She could feel the power of the Red Dragon surging through her. Feel the witch's magic pulsing darkly. She looked up at the winter-bare fruit trees in the orchard, but their limbs were sagging and catching fire at the tips.

I don't want to do this.

"Pack the snow against her skin," Nox murmured.

"You're burned," Torren said.

"It'll heal. Just pack her with snow, and we'll put her in the back of the truck. There's no time! Look at the smoke. He's gonna torch the orchard."

Torren muttered a curse.

"Help him," Riyah pleaded. Because she could feel the agony now. The veil between them was burned to ashes, and she could feel his heartbreak. It was just as potent as her own.

I don't want to do this.

And everything in her wanted to tell him, "Then don't. Come home to me." But what would that solve? Whatever the consequences, the Red Dragon needed to accept the loss of his offspring, and Vyr needed to mourn the passing of his sons.

Like she had. Pay homage to their too-short lives

and honor them by remembering them for always. He would keep their ghosts here, haunting the orchard, if he didn't let them go, but they deserved better. He did, too.

In the orchard, she stood and walked through the waves of heat until the toes of her boots were just feet away from the little graves.

The slamming of truck doors sounded, then a barked order from Nox. "Cut through the woods. No time to get to the main road."

The relief on her skin was fading, replaced by blistering heat again. Was this what it was like for Vyr? Every Change burned like he was standing in a fire? How could he endure this?

She was clenching her teeth, trying not to cry out.

There was no more snow that she could see. It was all melted. She fell to her knees in the mud. *I wanted to save you*, Vyr said in her mind. *I'm your father, and it was my job to keep you safe. To keep your mother safe. But I put dragons in you instead.* His voice sounded so thick, so heartbroken. *I'm sorry.*

Tears burned trails down Riyah's cheeks. She could feel the hate inside of Vyr. Hate for himself. She could feel everything. All the pain. The drive to claim more and more territory just so he didn't have to think about the loss. The need to hurt anyone who came after the people he cared about. The relentless urge to hunt, burn, and devour, because that's what injured animals did—they lashed out. And the injury in Vyr consumed his entire heart.

Everything he hadn't been able to put into words over the past six months was laid bare before her.

"Hurry," she whispered.

"We're almost there," Nox murmured.

Her body felt jolted over and over. Where was she? The bed of Torren's truck? All she could see was through Vyr's eyes in the orchard—heat waves and gravestones.

Isaac Daye

Farion Daye

A picture of a little dragon was etched under both names.

Her hands...Vyr's hands...traced them, and a single tear fell onto the stone surface of Isaac's. It sizzled and evaporated in an instant.

"I'm sorry," he choked out again.

And then agony rippled through her, bowing her body. She looked up to the sky. The only thing that would make her feel better was the mist of clouds against his scales, and releasing the fire in his belly, and devouring ashes.

The Red Dragon was coming.

"Vyr!" Riyah screamed as she was thrown from his mind.

She struggled for breath as she opened her eyes. She was lying in the back of Torren's truck, and Nox was hovering over her, his hand resting on her shoulder, his other on the edge of the bed, his eyes up ahead to wherever Torren was driving. Her body jostled hard as they hit a bump, then another.

"Ooooh, mother fuck cakes," Nox murmured, his eyes going wide.

Riyah struggled upright, but she already knew what she would see. She'd felt his Change coming, felt the Red Dragon clawing out of Vyr, burning him up from the inside out.

Smoke clung to the woods like fog, and she could see the distinct line where the snow had melted from whatever was happening to Vyr. The thick tires blasted right through three-inch thick snow to mud.

"Hold on!" Torren yelled out the open window, the back end of his truck fishtailing this way and that as he blasted through the woods, dodging sturdy pines.

Above the trees rose the fire-red spikes along the back of the Red Dragon.

"Oh, my gosh, Nox!" Riyah yelled. "What if he burns the sawmill?" He'd bought Torren a sawmill long ago, and the Crew had just got it up and running a year ago. That was their main income.

"He won't."

"How do you know?" she cried as the Red Dragon lifted his long neck and bellowed a roar into the sky. "We haven't called the other dragons. Who is here to stop him this time? We haven't even told Kane or Damon or—"

"Riyah!" Nox gritted out, gripping her shoulders. They jerked hard to the side, braced on their splayed knees. "Quit acting like a damn princess when we all know you're a dragon slayer."

"W-what?"

"I burned my beautiful bronzed skin to bring you here, woman. Wiggle your fingers and turn him into a turd or something."

"That's not how my powers work."

"I just saw you motherfuckin' levitate. Off the

ground. Like a ghost. Bing bong, clip clop, witch! Blink hard, point your magic wand, and stop the fire."

"Oh...just...stop the fire. You're stupid."

"You're stupid."

She yelped as Torren hit a big bump. Her knees were going to be black and blue, and indeed Nox's hair was mussed and his cheeks flushed. His sweater had been burned to tatters, exposing raw, red skin underneath. Whoops. They both gripped onto the sides of the truck for stability as the dragon beat his wings and created hurricane winds.

"You're stupid because you let me burn you," she muttered.

"Well, you're stupid because you bone a man-eating dragon."

"Well, you're stupid because last week I caught you eating cereal with orange juice."

"Well, you're stupid because you forgot to buy the milk so I had to eat the cereal—"

"Both of you, shut up!" Torren bellowed.

The Red Dragon spewed fire and lava in a line toward the east.

Nox muttered, "Torren is extra stupid because he's driving us right toward the Red Dragon's mouth."

"The stupidest," Riyah murmured, biting back a smile. This should not be funny, but something was changing for her lately. Maybe she was healing from everything, feeling better, appreciating the Crew for sticking with her when she'd lost her shit for half a year. It was nice to trade insults with Nox again. It felt like old times.

And watching her mate's power, even though it was born of pain, well, it made her proud. He'd done this to himself on purpose, knowing the consequences, knowing he wouldn't be able to keep the dragon in check, but he was trying to cope and catch up with her in their healing process anyway. Good mate for at least trying.

Those charitable thoughts lasted until Torren drove them through the last grove of wild foliage before they reached the perfect rows of fruit trees in the orchard. They were all on fire.

Fire was everywhere. He was hovering over the gravestones, spewing lava around him.

"Why isn't he airborne?" Nox asked over the sound of the engine.

"Because the dragon is protecting the babies."

"Protecting them from what?" Nox snarled.

Riyah shook her head helplessly. "I don't know. He's blocked me out again."

"Okay, you know what?" Nox yelled. "That's enough!"

Torren skidded to the side in front of the dragon and sped down a row of flaming trees, but Nox stood and jumped out. Just...jumped.

"Nox!" Riyah screamed.

"Shit," Torren said, barely audible above the sound of his truck. He slammed on the brakes, but Riyah was scrambling out before it even rocked to a stop. Nox stomped up to the dragon, splayed his legs, and yelled, "Hey, twatwagon!" Nox choked on the thick smoke, coughed a few times and then yelled, "You aren't the only one who lost them, you know!"

Vyr narrowed his eyes then opened his mouth full of razor-sharp teeth and blew fire at Nox.

Without thinking, Riyah yelped and held out her hands. She let the power pulse through her fingertips. The fire stopped just short of Nox, but Vyr wasn't letting up. Flames and lava spewed straight at Nox in an unending barrage. Torren's massive silverback ran past her toward the blond troublemaker, blocking him from Vyr. Great, now she had two idiots to shield from a pissed off dragon.

Vyr stopped his fire and inhaled again, his Firestarter clicking, but Nox called up to the monster, "You think you're the only one hurting? I wanted them, too! Nevada wanted them, too! We stopped trying for a baby because we thought between Dane and your twins, we would have plenty of little ones to spoil rotten! I had plans, you overgrown lizard! I was going to train them to love me more than you! I bought them custom-made onesies that said 'My uncle is hotter than your uncle!' I made a nursery for them, so we could have them for slumber parties! Sure, we all live in the same house and their nursery was in my closet, but it counted! I'm sad, too!" The last three words, he screamed at the top of his lungs.

"Me, too," Torren rumbled in his deep, inhuman voice. It was still a little freaky that he could talk in animal form.

"You greedy grunt," Nox yelled. "You think all the pain is yours? Well, it's not. We're all hurting. And instead of leaning on us, you pulled dick moves, pushed us all away, and you're making everything worse. I'm very angry at you! My therapist, aka

Nevada, told me I need to say my feelings, so there it is!"

The dragon sat there, poised protectively over the little graves, coiled to strike like a snake, glaring at Nox, smoke wafting from his nostrils.

"I think you're being a giant dick!" Nox screamed. "And since you burned your mate's orchard, she'll probably never give you another sixty-nine again!"

"That's not true," Riyah corrected, still holding her hands up in case the boys needed her protection. "Selfishly, I'm still all in on sixty-nines, but you *will* be re-planting my beautiful orchard, Vyr Daye! You made this place a sanctuary, and now you made it smell like smoke. You burned all my trees! I love you very much, but right now I don't like you."

The dragon's nostrils flared, and he huffed out a steaming breath as he looked around at the trees and mud and ash.

"Yeah, you cretin, you did that! To your own mate's gift that *you* gave her!" Nox yelled. "You're terrible!"

"Well," Torren growled, "not terrible. I sat on the model train I made for Dane, and that doesn't make me a bad person."

"Oh, my God," Nox belted out, turning to glare at Torren. "Don't make this about you."

"It's just that a person can carry a lot of guilt for stuff like this—"

"I'm gonna turn into a fuckin' bear, and I'm gonna eat you," Nox growled, shoving the silverback gorilla in the shoulder. "And then I'm gonna concentrate real hard and turn you into bunny poops. You know, like the pellets? And I'm gonna poop one pellet out at a time and name them each Torren the Terrible—"

Torren shoved Nox in the chest. "Nevada told you to stop talking about poop."

The dragon rumbled, but mostly he just sounded annoyed. The boys ignored him and just kept arguing. Riyah pursed her lips against a smile. Vyr's terrifying silver dragon eyes locked onto her, and she cleared her throat and tried to be serious. "Everyone deals with loss their own way, but perhaps burning my sanctuary isn't polite."

"You know what else isn't polite?" Nox punched his hands on his hips and arched his neck all the way back to look at the dragon.. "You taking over your mate's mind, setting her skin on fire, and her burning my nipples off. Look at this!" He pulled away the

167

burned, tattered shirt and exposed his torso. "They will heal because I'm a genetic miracle, and I'll probably look better than ever, but for the next three days, you have deprived my mate of nibbling on my nips."

"Ew," Torren said, his gorilla face all scrunched up in disgust.

"Bright side, she basically waxed my chest," Nox muttered, staring down at himself and rubbing his pecs.

Vyr let of a smoky dragon sigh, bunched his muscles, and outstretched his tattered, massive red wings. When he launched himself into the air, Riyah and Nox fell to their knees and Torren had to splay his powerful legs and arms under the force of the wind.

"Vyr!" Torren called after him.

"It's okay," Riyah said breathlessly. She closed her eyes so she could see through Vyr again. The burning orchard was growing smaller beneath her. "He's let me into his head. He's okay. Just needs to fly for a while. The dragon needs to think."

She opened her eyes to find Nox staring at her like she'd sprouted a pig nose. "What?"

"He just needs to fly? Have you not paid attention for the last six months? Vyr doesn't just fly anymore. He burns shit down. I mean...it's awesome, but we have to keep paying for the damages."

"By we, you mean Vyr. You don't make that much," Torren deadpanned.

"Then give me a raise, asshole, and maybe I could help pay for all the smiting and pillaging and burning."

He crawled over to Torren and shoved him again, then rose and began to walk off. But Torren reached out his massive arm and clipped his legs out from under Nox so he went down in the mud face-first. Torren stepped on his back as he made his way toward the truck. Nox's body made a squishing sound, and he grunted under Torren's weight.

"I'm telling Nevada you talked about poop again," Torren muttered.

Nox peeled himself from the mud. "I'm going to build Dane a model train that I don't sit on with my big clumsy ass, and then I'm going to train him to call me 'Dad.'"

"Do that and I'll kill you," Torren called over his shoulder.

"Poop. Pellets!"

Riyah waved her hands in front of her face to clear the smoke and coughed as she watched Vyr disappear into the clouds. She missed him already and hoped he came home soon. She made her way to the headstones and then wiped ashes off them with her hand. He'd burned their sanctuary, but it wasn't his fault. His anguish had just been too much.

Tomorrow they would go to the Oregon mountains to make their apologies to Grim and his Crew. She sighed heavily, trying to imagine how it would be. This would be the first time she ever left her babies.

It was time, though.

She had to get back to living.

She had to get back to keeping Vyr steady.

Because no matter what happened, they were in this life-thing together.

SEVEN

The dragon had landed a damned mile away from the house, and now Vyr was having to tromp all the way home, bare-ass naked and freezing cold. His dragon didn't much like the cold. It made him slower, and the Changes didn't last as long, but from the look of the sun setting on the horizon, he'd been away for several hours.

Rubbing his arms to put some warmth back into them, he stepped into the clearing and sighed in relief at seeing the mansion. From here, he could see a fire in the hearth through the sprawling front windows, but that wasn't the sight that settled his dragon. It was Riyah, sitting on the front porch swing, bundled in a blanket, cupping a metal thermos in her hands.

She wore a red beanie that matched her rosy cheeks and made her dark freckles stand out even more than usual. Her dark hair was in waves down her shoulders, and when she saw him, her full lips curved up in an uncertain smile. She waved at him.

He was exhausted down to his bones, frozen straight through, every muscle sore from the Change, and his skin felt raw and burned, but he still had some work to do.

When he made his way to the porch, she was holding out her arms with the corners of the blanket hooked in her hands.

He slipped right into her hug and allowed her to wrap the warm fabric around his shoulders. She was so warm and smelled like herbs. "Have you been mixing something up?" he asked. He'd built her a greenhouse where she could grow and dry plants to make the old salves she remembered from her mother.

"Something to heal our skin faster. That was a rough Change."

Vyr eased back and tugged at the V-neck of her sweater. Her skin was pink, and she winced when he touched her. "I've never dragged you through one before. Never kept you in my mind when it happened. I couldn't—"

"You couldn't help it." She leaned up and kissed him so sweetly he tugged her closer. "You did good. I watched the news but didn't see any footage of you burning any towns."

"I didn't burn anything. Didn't feel like it. I just wanted to be in the sky for a while. Riyah?"

Yes? she asked in his mind.

He smiled and hugged her tenderly so he wouldn't hurt her skin. *I'm sorry I wasn't there. I saw how it was for you, in your mind. You lost your parents, and you were hurt for a long time over it, but I saw it. I felt it. You've never felt more abandoned than you did these last six months. And it was me, the one who loves you the most, who made you feel alone. None of it was your fault, you know?*

It was.

No. His denial was so stern she couldn't argue if she tried. *You grew our babies so well. You took care of them in every way you could. Their little dragons were just too strong. Too impatient. It isn't anyone's fault. Not yours and not theirs.*

And not yours.

Vyr sighed and eased back, just far enough to cup her cheeks and look her into her eyes. "That part I'm going to try and accept because blaming myself for what happened isn't helping anything."

"Just love them, Vyr. Love them for those beautiful moments you felt them moving in my belly. That's all the time we were allowed to have with them." Riyah's breath hitched, and she ducked her gaze, lowered her chin to her chest. And when he eased her face back up, her eyes were rimmed with tears. She tried to smile anyway, tough mate. Beautiful badass.

"I'll do better. And I'll go with you to visit them now. I'll sit with you on that bench and talk to them with you. I saw it in your head. All the times you told them about the things you love most about their father. About me. Even when I didn't deserve for you to say anything nice. I'll replant your orchard, not just for you, but for them, too. And I'll apologize to Grim. I'll hate every second of it, but if you think that'll help Torren and Nox, then I'll do it."

"Really?"

"Grim made this Christmas wish to be a better Alpha, and it replays over and over in my head. He's broken, but he still has the drive to take care of his people. This year was the hardest on me, but maybe I could make a wish for next year. Maybe I can wish to be a better Alpha, too."

Riyah parted her pretty lips to say something, but her face was confiscated by a frown and the words stayed lodged in her throat as she stared at something behind him.

When he turned, Nox was headed this way, humming a song around a beef jerky stick, dragging what looked like a horse saddle with an extremely long cinch strap trailing behind him through the snow.

He looked up at Vyr and stopped in his tracks, his eyes round. Just buckled his legs and skidded to a stop. "Uuuuh, you're back early."

"What the fuck is that?" Vyr asked.

"What's what?" Nox answered innocently.

Vyr counted to three in his head so he wouldn't cuss ob-Nox-ious out. "The saddle you are holding in front of you."

Nox looked down like he'd never seen before in his life the thing he clenched in his hands. "Oh. This thing. Weeeeell...it's a saddle."

"For?"

"For our flight."

Vyr pursed his lips. Maybe he should just burn him and eat him. Just a little burning and eating. Just a little.

"Is that a dragon saddle?" Riyah asked, pointing to the cinch that was trailing in the snow yards behind Nox.

He looked behind him and said, "So, what of it? Maybe I spent three weeks making a custom dragon saddle. I think I should be the first one to ride the Red Dragon because I'm his best friend—"

"Torren is my best friend—"

"Torren barely likes you right now and, besides, I can watch your back and like...throw water balloons at people who try to take video of you, and steer you, and keep you from setting everything on fire." The words tumbled over each other as he blurted them out without taking a single breath.

Apparently Nox had been thinking about this a lot.

Vyr stood frozen for a four-count and then said, "I simply can't." He strode inside and let the swinging door close loudly behind him.

"So, is that a no to flying together to Grim's Mountains?" Nox called.

"We're taking a plane!" Vyr yelled.

"I never get to do anything fun!" Nox screamed. And then there was a huge thud as the saddle hit the side of the house.

He would've ignored the sound of giggling coming from the front porch, but those sounds belonged to Riyah. Vyr stilled by the hearth at the tinkling sound. It was music to a heart that hadn't heard any in a long time. God, Riyah was the least fragile person he'd ever met.

She walked through the door, a laugh still curving her lips, shaking her head as she dragged the blanket in. And when she looked up to see Vyr, the corners of her eyes crinkled with her smile.

There was his Riyah.

"Come here," he murmured.

She wasn't slow about it. She was playful, like the old them. She bolted to him and jumped, landing in his arms, the thermos in her hand sloshing as she threw her arms around his neck. "Take me on a date in Tillamook," she said lightly. "I hear they have a cheese factory that does tours, and they sell ice cream there and everything. I love cheese and ice cream."

Vyr chuckled, kissed her, and then sucked on her bottom lip before he sat on the couch, taking her with him.

"If it's going to be just me and you, no kiddos of our own, I want you to date the shit out of me and keep me nice and distracted."

"Mmmm," he said as she wiggled her pelvis against his erection. "Distracted how?"

"With naked parties."

"Naked parties, cheese, and ice cream. I think I can manage that." *Anything to make you happy.*

She smiled as he put the last words into her mind. *And anything to make you happy, too. I love you, Vyr Daye.*

I love you always, Riyah Daye.

She nodded once. "Then it's settled. Date night. I want to go to dinner somewhere new. In Grim's Mountains." She nuzzled her cheek against his and admitted softly, "I think it'll be good for us to get away from here for a little while together."

"Agreed," Nox muttered.

Vyr looked over Riyah's shoulder and glared at Nox, who had somehow snuck in here, still eating his beef jerky stick as he leaned on the counter in the kitchen.

"You aren't coming on date night."

"That's what she said," Nox uttered with a snort.

Vyr considered throwing Riyah's thermos at his face.

Riyah laughed and hugged the metal canister to her chest, then shook her head slightly. He'd forgotten she was still in his head. He was going to have to get used to it all over again, but that was okay. He didn't want the wall between them ever again. Good or bad thoughts, he wanted to share everything with his mate.

She made him feel better. And not just like healing-from-a-cold feel better or recovering-from-a-bad-Change feel better. She made his soul feel like it could be okay again. He'd gone dark inside, but she was still here, still light, still sharing that good magic, that love, with him. It didn't matter that he wasn't worthy of it. All that mattered was that this woman loved him unconditionally and was still here, fighting right alongside him.

If she could find the grit to smile and laugh after everything she'd been through, then he had no right to keep spiraling.

For the first time in a long time, he was looking forward to traveling because, this time, it wasn't something his dragon was forcing him to do. It was a trip with his Crew and a night out with his mate, a chance to make her feel loved, like she made him feel.

He was one lucky sonofabitch to have somehow gained the loyalty of this Crew. And even luckier still to have earned the love of the woman smiling at him like he hung the moon.

Once upon a time, in the shifter prison where they'd met, Riyah had told him, "I'll be your star. I believe in you. I'll wait with you while better things are coming." And she hadn't quit on him. Not once, not even for a moment. Her loyal heart had chosen him, and that was that. And somewhere along the way, he'd become her star, too.

The thing about being someone's star, though...that star owed a debt. If someone believed in it that much, the least it could do was keep shining.

So here was his moment, on the day he'd visited his little dragons' graves for the first time, on the day his Crew had come to stop him from burning the orchard, on the day he'd accepted that his mate wasn't going anywhere, no matter how far he fell or how unrecognizable he became on his insides... This was the moment he found his grit like Riyah had done. No matter the effort it took, he was going to turn this around and bring the Red Dragon back under control.

No. More. Mountain ranges.

The world deserved for him to stop claiming them.

And his people deserved to have him home.

EIGHT

Nox leaned over the first-class seat and shoved a list in front of Vyr's face. "I've made an itinerary for our trip."

Riyah giggled to herself. Oh, she couldn't wait to see what he'd added to it.

Vyr scrunched up his face as he read it aloud. "One, cheese factory. B, see Oregon's grade-A, grass-fed moo cows. Three, kill and eat moo cows. Four, I'm a bear shifter, stop looking at the list like it's weird. E, apologize to Remington, Juno, and Ash for being mega-dicks and trying to kill them and their mates. Six, make Nox Second in the Crew. Seven, lose Torren in the Oregon mountains somewhere because he is boring. Eight, give Nox all your beers on the flight."

"Ow," Nox muttered as Torren smacked him in the back of the head.

"All the drinks are free in first class, you idiot," the grumpy silverback shifter pointed out. "And I'm not boring. I'm just sick of all of your perverted jokes today. If I hear you say 'that's what she said' one more time, I'm going to break that window and shove you through it. I keep thinking if I just ignore you, you will stop trying to annoy everyone and be quiet. But no, the more we ignore you, the more obnoxious you are."

"I'll never give up," Nox muttered. He turned to the passing flight attendant and smiled sweetly. "Can I have two Bud Lights?" He leaned over Vyr and Riyah's seats again. "Why didn't you get our seats all in a row so we could look at each other?"

"So I don't have to look at you," Vyr muttered, leaning his head back and closing his eyes.

"Want to play I-spy?" Nox asked.

Vyr was currently giving Riyah very vivid imagery of him helping Torren throw Nox off the plane, and the smile growing on his face was a little disturbing.

Hoping to save Nox's life, Riyah asked Nox,

"Aren't you supposed to be buckled?"

"I can't figure out the Wi-Fi," Nox murmured, poking at his phone. "I promised Nevada I would send her a dick pic from the plane, but it won't let me buy service."

"I'm sure Nevada will survive," Vyr said without opening his eyes. Now he was imagining eating Nox whole while he was a dragon.

"Clearly, you don't understand our dynamics. Nevada is seven levels out of my league, and the biggest thing I have going for me is my dick. I have to keep her addicted to it, even when I'm traveling, so that she never feels neglected and only thinks of me and what I can do to her body twenty-four-seven. I even manscaped."

Riyah had turned in her seat, watching Nox through the crack between their chairs. She whispered to her mate, "You've never sent me a dick pic. I feel a little cheated."

"There, I got the internet." Nox started unsnapping the top button of his jeans like he would take the picture right then and there, but Torren slapped his hand away from his crotch and confiscated his phone. They broke out in a scuffle, but mostly were just slapping at each other like two giant, tattooed, grown-ass siblings in the back seat of a long car ride.

Riyah faced forward again. She reached for his mind. *I think I want a dick pic!*

The little headache that said Vyr was deep in her head started just behind her eyes. Most people didn't like headaches, but she did. She liked being this close to Vyr.

You see my dick all the time.

But I want pictures. So I can bring it up and stare at it and miss your dick when you aren't with me.

Vyr opened his eyes and rolled his head toward her. The fight behind Nox and Torren was getting louder, but they both were professionals at ignoring them. *Seriously? Most girls don't want dick pics.*

Riyah gave him her sexiest crooked smirk. "Well, there's your first problem, thinking I'm like other girls."

"Oh, woman, I would never mistake you for that. You are one of a kind." *You want a dick pic? You got it. I'm gonna send it to you at some random time when you are supposed to be serious, though, so you blush and stutter and get busted with a naughty grin on your face.*

Riyah giggled and pulled her knees up to her chest. "I like this game." *I'll send you boobie pics, too.*

The wicked expression on Vyr's face vanished. "Yes, please." *You are the best wife and the best mate and have the prettiest tits in the whole world*, he said loudly in his head.

And now heat was creeping into her cheeks. That was the best compliment he'd given her in a long time, so she rewarded him with touch because Vyr did better with affection now. She wrapped her arms around his stony bicep, rested her cheek against his shoulder, and smiled at the chick-flick movie he'd let her choose for them to watch together.

The rest of the flight went by fast. The boys quieted their arguing when they had beers to occupy them, and Riyah fell asleep against Vyr's arm. When she woke, the pilot was instructing the flight attendants to prepare for landing, and then it was only another half hour before they were earthbound again.

Vyr had rented them the biggest SUV he could, thank goodness, because Torren needed space from Nox by the time they were an hour into the drive to the mountains near Tillamook, Oregon. He took up the entire third row, sat right in the middle, massive arms draped over the seats, glaring straight ahead. In the middle seat, Nox kept swatting at the back of his own neck, but that was probably because of the rumbling noise coming from Torren and his bright green gorilla eyes. Riyah tried to help by turning the music up louder to drown out the aggressive animal sounds, but their snarling ramped up even noisier. He was getting her inner polar bear all riled up, too. She was only a couple years Turned, while in the same shifter prison she'd met Vyr, and sometimes she didn't have the best control.

"Torren," Vyr growled, ghosting a glance at him in the rearview mirror, "if you make Riyah Change, I'm gonna burn you."

"Need. Food," Torren grunted in a gravelly voice. Hangry wasn't even a big enough word for what happened to these boys when they got their hunger pangs.

So they pulled over and got lunch at a hole-in-the-wall burger joint.

"Have you let Grim know we're coming?" she asked as they sat down with their food.

"No," Vyr murmured. I would rather catch them in their natural habitat."

"He means he would rather catch them fucking up than warning them the boss is coming so they pretend to be working like a well-oiled machine," Nox called across the room around a giant bite of food in his mouth. He and Torren had opted to sit at a different table, as far away from Vyr as they could get.

"I've always respected that about you, you know?" she said softly, tearing one of her French fries into tiny pieces.

"What?" Vyr asked.

"You were never one for perfection. You prefer real. Your father reacts well when he sees professionalism, but with your mountains, you don't put pressure on the Crews."

"Pressure on them won't turn these shifters to diamonds. It will just crush them," Vyr said.

"But you recognize that. You let them improve on their own. Or not. Their future and how far they get is up to them. You just provide a safe place for them to recover."

He was so handsome in this light. They were

sitting by a big front window, and the sunshine was hitting his face just right. His bright silver eyes were made even brighter by the saturated light. The tendrils of tattoo ink that curled out from under the sleeves of his T-shirt were stark against his smooth, pale skin. The light and shadows highlighted and smudged the curves of his muscles like some charcoal drawing in a gallery. He was soooo...Vyr.

"That was the compromise I could live with," he murmured, staring at his food. This was an admission. She could feel it. They hadn't talked much in the last six months while they were both spiraling in their own little worlds.

"The compromise you made with the Red Dragon?"

He nodded. "I don't have much control anymore. He wants to claim everything, but if I put a Last Chance Crew on the mountains I claim and give them a shot at recovering, I can feel like I did something good, you know?" He looked up at her with those striking silver snake eyes.

"You're a good man, you know?"

Vyr huffed a laugh and shook his head. "Woman, you've been drinking."

"Oh, please, I had one glass of wine on the plane, and that was hours ago. I know you, Vyr Daye. I know your heart. I can see inside your head whether you're quiet and thoughtful or the dragon is raging. You never stop trying. You never have that 'fuck it, just go burn everything' moment. It's not in you to quit. Torren is your guardian. And I'm your guardian. That's what people say. But they don't realize the real guardian of the Red Dragon. The one who does all the quiet work and saves the world every day? It's you, Vyr. You're a badass. And I know you get tired. I can feel it now. You're exhausted. But I'm here. You can lean on me."

"I'm also here," Nox said from across the restaurant.

Vyr twisted in his seat to look at the boys, the legs of his metal chair scraping the tile floor.

Riyah waited for the punchline to Nox's joke because he always had a punchline, but the blond-haired, beefed-up, tattooed jokester stared back at Vyr with the most solemn expression she'd ever seen on his face.

Torren was leaning on his elbows, hands clasped in front of him, empty plate pushed away, frowning as he studied Vyr. "I didn't know that was why you've been putting those fuck-up Crews in the territory you claim."

Vyr shook his head. "It's not some big honorable thing—"

"Yes, it is," Torren said so softly she almost missed it. "I thought it was part of your need to control people, but I was wrong. This whole time I thought you were just making more Crews to put under you." Torren swallowed hard. "I thought we weren't enough."

Vyr huffed a breath and stood. He hesitated a moment and then grabbed his and Riyah's plates before making his way to their table. He sat by Torren and then waited until Riyah took her seat next to Nox before he spoke. "The Sons of Beasts have always been enough. The dragon wants territory, not Crews. My dad keeps tabs on every shifter in existence. It's always been his instinct. He stopped trying to claim territory a long time ago, but he still watches everyone. For me, I do that on a smaller scale. I watch the outcasts, the ones I relate to. The ones who struggle like I do, or like you, Torren, or like you, Nox. Like Candace and Nevada." He looked at her and gave a small, crooked smile. "Like Riyah, the ones who have trouble finding their place in this world. It feels good to give them homes. The dragon doesn't give a shit about that part, but I do. There's good and bad in all of us, but some have to fight harder against the bad. I want those to succeed so at the end of my life, I can look back and not just see the fires I set. I want to be able to look back on the fires I put out, too."

For every bridge Vyr had been burning, secretly, he'd been building new ones.

Torren cleared his throat once...twice. "I'm here, too."

Those three words welded together one of the many cracks in the Sons of Beasts Crew.

Oh, the scar would still be there, but it wasn't bleeding anymore.

Under the table, Riyah slid her ankles against her mate's. *Good Alpha.*

Vyr offered her a slow, crooked smile. Her favorite.

There he was—her Vyr.

And this was the moment she knew he'd been right.

Everything would be okay.

NINE

Riyah had never been to these mountains. Vyr had talked about them before, and she'd tried to imagine them, but never had she come close to the real thing.

Oregon was beautiful. They'd taken winding roads through logging territory to get to Grim's Mountains. Entire forests had been cut and re-planted in sections, each with signs telling passersby the date the trees were replanted. On the way, they'd passed two lumberyards with towering stacks of logs that reminded her of home.

Vyr turned and offered Riyah his hand on the last ridge. The parking area was farther down the mountain, and they'd had to follow a trail to the

Rogue Pride Crew's trailer park.

The woods they were hiking through were covered in pine and ferns, moss and wild grasses. Evergreen needles blanketed the earth, and the woods smelled of rich, wet dirt, tree sap, and...smoke.

Something zinged past Vyr and slammed into the tree right beside him.

Riyah gasped as the fire-tipped arrow smoked and vibrated from the force of hitting the tree.

"You missed," Vyr said in a bored voice to a tall, lanky man with Rockstar hair and gold eyes.

He was standing in the middle of the clearing, dipping the tip of another arrow into the firepit. "It was a purposeful miss, Dragon," he said. "The first was a warning. The next will be a skull shot. I hear your healing is faster than us normie shifters. We'll see if you can re-grow a face."

"Vyr?" Ashlynn Kane asked, stepping down a set of porch stairs toward them.

Beaston Novak's daughter, Remington, and Brighton Beck's daughter, Juno, stepped out of the trailer behind Ashlynn, the one with the numbers 1010 beside the door. The women were all wearing sweater dresses and boots.

Riyah had met the girls in this Crew during holidays in Damon's Mountains. Before the Sons of Beasts had gone to war with the Daughters of Beasts.

All three of them looked utterly stunned as they made their way slowly toward Riyah and the boys.

"We have a good thing here," Juno said. "If you're here to take it away, we aren't going down quietly."

"He's good," Ash said in a soft voice. "Vyr is good. I can tell. He's been messing up, but he's still Vyr."

Riyah slid her hands up his bicep as Torren and Nox came to stand on either side of them. "We aren't here for trouble," Riyah said.

"Then why are you here?" a woman with long silver hair asked from where she stood on the porch of the last singlewide mobile home.

"Rose," Vyr greeted her with a nod.

"Red Dragon," she said formally. "My grandson is working near here with Kamp. He's close."

Riyah didn't miss the warning in the woman's voice.

"If I wanted Grim or any of you dead, you wouldn't be standing here," Vyr said simply. "Grim is safe from me."

"Ya damn right, he is," said the man loading a

fiery arrow.

"Rhett," Juno whispered with a frown.

Rose spoke up, "Did you buy my plane ticket here so that I would be safely away from Tarian Pride territory when you took it over? I've been wondering that for the last week. I think you care about Grim and his people. I think." She frowned. "You're hard to figure out. You burned half of my home mountains, and then you paid for me to be with my grandson and his Crew for the holidays. Was it out of guilt? Or are you planning more war?"

Vyr smiled wickedly. "Clever Rose. The thought did cross my mind to take the territory while you are here. Grim and all of you would've stayed out of it if you were safely away."

"Because you don't want to hurt us," Ash said. "You smile like you got the devil in you, but you're trying to make your wicked deeds less wicked, Vyr. You're trying to get your people out of the way before your dragon is bad again, aren't you?"

Vyr's smirk fell from his face, and he composed it like his father so often did into an unreadable mask. He placed his hands behind his back and asked, "When will Grim be back?"

"Grim? Not for a while," Rhett said, leaning on the hip-height compound bow. "The Reaper, though, he's here right now."

And right at that moment, a monstrous, black-maned, golden-eyed, scarred-up lion came barreling out of the woods straight for them. His muscles rippled as he charged, and his lips were curled back to expose long, curved canines. He looked terrifying.

One moment was all it took for Vyr to lose control.

One moment, and Riyah could see it so clearly in his head. That loss of himself wasn't because the Reaper was coming for Vyr. It was because he was aiming his hostility in the general direction of Riyah, Nox, and Torren. And the Red Dragon, for all his faults, loved his Crew as much as a monster could love. And he would burn anyone who threatened them.

Vyr gritted out a pained noise, then bunched his muscles and jumped impossibly high into the air. The ground around his feet had sunk in and cracked from the force. The dragon exploded from his body at the height of his leap, near the top of the forest canopy. Wind whooshed down upon them all, flattening them against the ground.

He beat his scarred and ripped red wings hard, aiming for the clouds, and when he reached them, he twisted in the air and dove, circling back for them. The Reaper had been pushed to the side with the force of Vyr's Change, but began his charge again for Nox and Torren and Riyah. Another lion, Kamp, she guessed, came fast from the woods and slammed into the side of the Reaper just as Nox and Torren Changed.

The Red Dragon was coming for the Reaper. His eyes were narrowed on the lion, and she could hear his Firestarter clicking deep in his throat. The sound echoed through the mountains.

"Vyr!" she screamed. "Don't!"

Everything happened at once. Juno, Remington, and Ash Changed into grizzlies, Rhett and Rose into lions, and all of them headed straight for the Reaper. They weren't coming for war on the Sons of Beasts. They were coming to the aid of their Alpha...or perhaps to stop him. Or fight him. Yes, they were definitely going to fight him.

Riyah's inner bear roared to be released, and her skin tingled with the first signs of the Change, but she wouldn't be fast enough to do anything. She couldn't Change and get to the Reaper fast enough to protect them.

"Stop his fire," Torren's gorilla growled out before he bolted right for the divebombing dragon.

On the verge of a Change, Riyah lifted her hands, palms up, and focused every bit of her energy on Vyr and the Rogue Pride Crew. Her powers weren't an exact science, though, and the bear was feeding her power too fast. The adrenaline was doing something bad to her, and waves of sick power pulsed from her. When Vyr opened his mouth and blew fire, Riyah screamed and diverted it upward to keep the fire from the ground. He was so low to the ground. Time slowed as Torren blasted toward him, leapt off the ground with his arms outstretched, and gripped onto one of the small red spikes that lined the Red Dragon's jaw. Torren almost lost his grip when Vyr was catapulted upward with the force of her blast.

Nox roared as he stood protectively beside Riyah, but there was nothing to be done. Torren could hold on or fall. His destiny was completely up to his grip strength and the Red Dragon's reaction to the gorilla.

Torren held on with one hand as Vyr arched his

long back and pulled up toward the sky again.

He was going to fall. She could see it in Torren's eyes that he was losing his grip. *Red Dragon, it's Torren. Take care of him. He's yours!*

Riyah cast another pulse of power from her hands, but it didn't just go up. It levelled trees to her right with a deafening crash, but she couldn't worry about that right now. She was focused on pushing Torren upward to help him get a better grip. Gravity was not a friend to the silverback right now.

As Vyr turned sharply, she lost sight of the gorilla and waited on baited breath for him to fall. Nox was running in that direction as though he would try to catch him when he did, but Torren never fell off the Red Dragon. As seconds went on and nothing fell from the sky, she searched Vyr desperately, hoping he would turn enough so she could see Torren and make sure he was okay.

And when he did give her a glimpse of the gorilla still clinging to his face spikes, Torren was yelling something into the Red Dragon's ear hole.

Holy shit, he was doing it. The Red Dragon wasn't circling back. Whatever Torren was telling him, it was working. Riyah could feel the Red Dragon listening to him.

Nox Changed back into a very naked, very angry man. "Are you fucking kidding me? I can't ride him, but Torren can?"

If anything about this situation was funny, Riyah would've laughed. As it stood, though, Vyr was now burning a line in the valley between the mountains, the Reaper was still fighting his entire Crew, the girls' pretty dresses lay in tatters where they'd Changed, Nox was jamming both middle fingers at the sky, and Riyah's power had destroyed a good thirty yards of forest down the side of the mountain.

All they'd wanted to do was come here and apologize, and now look at this chaos.

Freakin' C-Teams.

But she was a bright side kind of shifter-witch, and on a positive note, the Red Dragon had gone protective over his Crew. He'd also listened to whatever reasoning Torren was screaming into his ear and hadn't burned down the trailer park and all its inhabitants. Those felt like small victories.

And with dragons, any victory, no matter how small, counted for a lot.

Good Alpha.

TEN

What was taking so long? It felt like hours since Vyr had re-burned the territory.

Grim and his Crew were inside the mobile home at the end, probably cleaning up after the fight. Some of them definitely needed stitches.

She was standing out by the firepit keeping warm, and beside her, Nox had dragged up a bright green plastic lawn chair that was held together with duct tape, like someone had thrown it against a tree or something.

More reminders of home, ha.

The flimsy chair legs were splayed in the dirt under Nox's weight, and beside him was a six pack of some kind of beer named Pen15 Juice. The font on the logo was unfortunate since it looked like it said PenIS Juice. She pursed her lips against a smile and snuggled deeper into her jacket. Clouds were covering up the sun now, and it made everything look and feel colder.

"What's wrong with him?" Rose asked softly as she approached from behind.

"Nothing," Nox answered without looking at her. He took a long drag of a beer and did the man-sigh afterward. "He's just an outlaw, and outlaws can't be tamed."

Rose came to stand on the other side of Riyah, holding her hands out to the fire to warm them. "I'm serious."

Riyah parted her lips to say something, but it was Nox who answered again, "He's a territorial dick, land-hungry, has a dragon he can't control, pyromaniac, multiple personalities, aggressive, mediocre Alpha, closed off when he's hurt, doesn't talk about feelings, can't stay in one place, and is the only person in the world who actually likes eating pea soup. Pros, he's best friends with me." Another swig of beer as Riyah stared down at him with her mouth hanging open. "Oh, and his mate is pretty cool, too." He winked and did a silent cheers, then whispered, "Manners. You bitches love compliments."

Riyah slapped him in the back of the head, and he spewed beer onto the fire. The flames leapt a little higher and then simmered down again.

"He's been hurting," Riyah said. "The dragon is hard enough to manage when everything is steady. When he suffers? It's ten times harder to keep him in control."

"What hurt?" Rose asked softly.

This was the part Riyah hated. The part where she was supposed to admit without breaking down that she'd lost her own children, that she hadn't been able to get them to air safely. She was still a work in progress on this part. Clearing her throat, she said as steady as she could, "We lost twins. It isn't our fate to have biological children. Their dragons were too strong too early."

"Oh, my God," Rose whispered. She hugged Riyah. "I'm so sorry for what you've both been through." The woman hugged her tighter. "When he came to burn Tarian Territory, I feared it was something bad that had happened to him that set him off, but my heart hurts that it's this. He deserves better. So do you. You both would've been amazing parents to those precious babies."

Riyah's heart stuttered as she melted into the woman's hug. She'd talked about this so little with outsiders. She stared at the sky, praying for strength not to break down. Because that's what happened, right? The pain never went away. A person could only hope to grow strong enough to hold the pain.

"Did you steal that from the shed?" Rhett asked.

Riyah released Rose and turned to find the Rogue Pride Crew all filing out of the trailer.

Nox lifted his beer up in the air. "I give it sixty-nine stars. Highly recommend."

"You could've given us a heads-up you were coming into my territory," said a tall, muscular, tatted-up man with a Mohawk. Grim. He came to stand beside Rose.

"You mean Vyr's territory," Nox said.

Grim let off a low growl. "The Reaper doesn't like surprises."

"Yeah," Riyah said understandingly, remembering Vyr's immediate reaction to Grim charging out of the woods. "Neither does the Red Dragon. I get it, and I'm sorry we didn't give you a call. Vyr didn't want you all on your best behavior. He wanted you…"

"All fighting each other?" Ash asked brightly. "Because we totally did that." She had a scratch across her cheek, but she didn't favor it when she grinned.

There was a loaded moment of silence, and then Juno let off a little giggle. And then Remington joined along with Ash. Kamp stood back, arms crossed over his chest, both him and Rhett fighting smiles.

Nox cleared his throat and stood. Riyah couldn't read his face as he looked from person to person, but he hesitated when he got to Juno. Slowly, he traced three long-healed claw marks on the side of her neck. When Rhett snarled, Nox dropped his hand back to his side. "Wasn't my choice," he murmured. "Torren and I never wanted to hurt any of you. We didn't know we were there to claim Tarian Pride territory."

"Nox Fuller," Ash whispered, stepping right up to him and wrapping her arms around his waist. "Did you just apologize?" She squeezed him hard until his back made a popping sound and said, "I never in a million years thought you would go soft!"

Riyah cracked up. This was awesome watching Nox's cheeks turn the shade of cherries. "His mate

207

has been teaching him manners." She scrunched up her face at him and repeated his words, "Bitches love compliments."

He glared at her, but pulled Juno in for a hug, and then Remington.

She could feel Vyr now. He was close. He still had the wall up between them, but it was thinning.

He and Torren strode out of the woods, both bare-ass naked, covering their nethers and damn near blue-skinned from the cold.

"'Scuse me," she said, stepping around the fire pit. She bolted for him. She'd been so worried! He caught her just as she launched herself into his arms, and Vyr hugged her so tightly. He buried his face against her neck and was making a purring sound she hadn't heard in months. The dragon was content. Thank God. "You did good," she whispered against his ear.

Torren was standing there, tall as a building, shivering. But his face looked different. He was smiling, and it had been a while since Riyah had seen that. And then he did something that shocked her. Torren winked at her and then made his way toward the others where he hugged up the girls and offered his hand to Grim to shake. They looked alike, two tattooed giants standing there in the evening shadows, one with gold eyes and one with green, both brawlers. The Reaper and the Kong. Riyah was suddenly filled with pride for her Crew. They could've gone their whole lives not making apologies for war. It was easier to not give a fuck. But they did the hard thing and made amends.

Grim broke from the crowd and strode for Riyah and Vyr. He was holding a pair of folded sweats and a hoodie. Vyr eased Riyah to the side and straightened his spine, lifted his chin.

The Alpha of Rogue Pride was growling a threatening sound, and his face was a study in ambivalence and uncertainty, but he handed Vyr the clothes and murmured, "Thanks for not burning us all to ashes." Grim cleared his throat and canted his head at Vyr, studied him. "And also thank you for letting us keep working in these mountains. It's...well, it's become home. I never thought I would feel that about a place, but you...you gave that to us."

Vyr ducked his chin once. "You're welcome."

Grim scratched his thick beard with his thumb and glanced back at his Crew. Ash, his mate, was looking at him with the mushiest smile. "We were heading into town to celebrate New Year's," Grim murmured. "It's why the girls were all dressed up. It's my grandma's last day with us, so we wanted to cut loose a little." Grim shifted his weight and cleared his throat. "Would you and your Crew like to stay for a while?"

Vyr first looked to Riyah, then back to Grim and nodded with shock pooling in his bright eyes. "We'd love that."

Two broken Alphas and both men of few words, but that didn't matter. It was so clear they understood each other, and more than that, they respected each other.

Riyah could see it now, why Vyr kept coming back here. Why he kept watching Grim. She could feel his relief when he was around him. Someone else like him existed. Someone who would never have full control over his animal side. But who, like Vyr, kept trying anyway.

And as she watched her Crew talking to Rogue Pride, dissipating memories of war between them with laughter, she could imagine another deep crack in her Crew being welded together.

And that's what healing was about. Mending one

fracture at a time until a bond could bear weight again.

They were doing the work, and they didn't need her protection from Vyr anymore. So, she closed her eyes and exhaled softly, lifted the shield she'd been blanketing them with for all these months. Torren and Nox had grown strong enough to stand on their own again and shoulder the bond with the biggest, baddest, most volatile dragon in the world.

When she opened her eyes, Torren and Nox had locked their attention on Vyr and wore matching smiles. And Vyr—*her* Vyr, because that's what he was again—stroked his fingers down her spine and nodded to Nox and Torren.

Everything is okay, he whispered through the bond. *I'll make everything okay. No matter what happens from here on, I'll never let us get broken like that again.*

Riyah slipped her hand into his and reached for his mind.

Good Alpha.

ELEVEN

"Dammit, Nox," Vyr growled, "get Mr. Diddles off the table."

The swan in question was standing over a plate of hot dog buns going to town like Cookie Monster. Bread crumbs were flying, and the swan was wagging his little stump tail like a happy golden retriever.

Nox flipped through a daily planner. "According to my daily planner, it's Torren's turn to deal with Mr. Diddle's shit."

Candace popped a french fry into her mouth and leaned over Nox's shoulder, squinting her eyes at his notebook. "All I see written in there is 'I love Nevada's tits' and a dick with a smiley face."

Vyr growled and removed the oversized feasting bird from the table himself. "I built him a castle. A castle! That swan has a mini-mansion, and yet he's spent the entire winter in here."

Torren set a plate of burger patties and hot dogs in the middle of the table. "I'll never get over you calling that bird Mr. Diddles in your fancy-as-fuck voice."

"There's a feather in my water," Vyr groused, plucking a white plume out gingerly.

Riyah giggled and rested her hand on his thigh when he sat down next to her. Three months, and everything was back to normal. The swan honked. Nox sat down too hard on his chair, the leg broke, and he busted his ass. Nevada laughed so hard she snorted. Torren downed an entire hot dog like some giant tattooed anaconda. Candace was yelling, "Yeah baby, one bite, you know how to turn me on." And Dane was a shifted baby gorilla, climbing up the curtains of the heavily windowed room.

Well...they were back to normal for them.

"You're quiet tonight," Vyr said low, leaning closer to her from his spot at the head of the table. "And you've had me shut out for a week, but you're sitting on the edge of your seat and grinning. Nervous. Excited. Nervous. Excited." He was studying her with his head canted to the side.

Riyah grinned. "I know something you don't know."

She felt the tingle of a headache right behind her eyes that told her Vyr was pushing harder to get into her mind. She closed the wall between them and shook her head. "Nuh uh uuuuuh. You'll ruin the surprise."

Vyr frowned, his ruddy eyebrows lowering over those bright blue eyes of his. The dragon color wasn't there quite as much anymore. Victory. "I don't much like surprises."

"I really think you'll like this one."

He looked so handsome in this light, his cheekbones chiseled, his eyes slightly slanted like a cat's. His face didn't look haunted anymore. He'd trimmed his beard shorter, and his arms and chest rippled against the thin fabric of his blue T-shirt. She'd always loved that color on him. Made his eyes pop. *Handsome, handsome mate.*

"Mmmmm, I heard that," he rumbled, sliding her hand to his lips.

"Eep!" She shut the wall down tighter so he wouldn't see into her memories. Over the past few months, the Sons of Beasts had grown closer to Rogue Pride. And for Riyah, she'd begun building a friendship with Ashlynn Kane, the mate of Grim. It was Ash and Grim who were about to change the entire course of Riyah and Vyr's lives.

When her phone buzzed, she glanced at the text that flashed across the screen. *Pulling up now.* It was from Grim.

Chills rippled up her spine, and tears were already burning her eyes just from those three words. This was really happening! She had an urge to pull up the picture Ash had sent her last week and look at it for the hundredth time. It was the boy from Beaston's vision. Ash and Grim had found him without even knowing Beaston's prediction, but Riyah had been so careful to hide him from Vyr in case something fell through. It had been a huge fear that her hopes would be shattered again. And if her heart was broken again, she wanted to protect Vyr from a broken heart, too.

Torren had been right in the middle of squirting a ridiculous amount of mustard onto a half dozen hot dogs when he froze. His bright green eyes narrowed, and the joke he was telling faded off mid-punchline. "Do you hear that?"

"Yeah, Dane is ripping the curtain to shreds," Candace muttered, making her way toward the little hellraising Kong.

"No, someone is coming."

"That's what she said," Nox muttered, sketching something into his journal with a piece of charcoal.

Torren gave him a look of pure annoyance.

"Yeeeesss," Nox said creepily, "hold that frown." He sketched faster.

"Are you drawing my face?" Torren griped, yanking the journal out of Nox's hands.

"Hey, give me back my dream journal!" He kicked the leg of Torren's chair so hard it busted, and the gorilla went down hard.

Riyah barely ducked out of the way fast enough when the notebook went sailing. The sound of shattering glass was deafening, and Nevada and Candace both yelled, "Seriously?"

Already, half the windows were held together with duct tape.

Vyr looked tired as he slow blinked at the newly

broken window and chewed a bite of cheeseburger. "I would tell you to pay for that, but we all know you're just going to use duct tape and buy beer instead."

"For all of us!" Nox said. "Because I'm the MVP. Every time you go to the fridge, there is a cold one in there just waiting for you. Beer trumps broken windows."

When Vyr closed his eyes and inhaled a steadying breath, Riyah took a peek into his mind. He was counting to ten, imagining a field of dandelions waving in the wind. Which seemed really peaceful except he was also imagining Nox tied to a chair in the middle of that field, covered in honey and bumble bees. He also had a black eye. Vyr smiled. And then his attention jerked to the window because the sound was getting louder. Torren had been right; there was the sound of a car engine.

They were really, really here.

Slowly, Riyah stood and watched as the navy-blue Ford Expedition with rental plates made its way up the circle drive. "Vyr, I…"

"What's wrong?" he asked, standing.

"Nothing is wrong," she whispered. "Something is *right*. And I think sometimes things happen for a reason. Even terrible things. That's the only way I've been able to make sense of what we went through. Feels like we went through a long storm, but now it's time for a rainbow." Her breath hitched as she slipped her hand into his. "I hope."

Vyr's eyes sparked with intensity as he looked from her to the car parking outside. "It's Grim and Rose." He swallowed hard. "And someone else. I can hear them." Realization came over his face in a wave. Pulling her, he made his way out the front door, the Sons of Beasts following behind them.

Grim was the first out of the SUV. "Vyr," Grim greeted him, clasping his hand, but Riyah only cared about greeting another. One small boy. A toddler. Two years old. A lion. Green eyes. Little brawler. Dragon-hearted.

She blinked back tears because nothing was settled. Nothing. If it wasn't meant to be, Grim and Rose would take the cub back to Ronin of the Tarian Pride. Her hope could still be demolished.

Rose got out, holding him—the boy from Beaston's vision.

Riyah's heart recognized him.

He was somber and curious, looking around,

clinging to Rose.

Riyah stepped away from Vyr and approached Rose and the little boy. "Hiiiiii," she whispered, trying to keep it together as she rubbed his little back. She could feel it. The feral little rumble that vibrated through his body. He was growling.

"This is Brayden," Rose murmured. Her eyes were rimmed with moisture. "We can't keep him."

"Why not?" Vyr asked in a careful tone. He stood with his hands clasped behind his back, expression unreadable, but every muscle in his body was tense, and his eyes swam with...something.

"His father was Justin Moore," Grim murmured, "the old Alpha of the Tarian Pride." His face twisted with fury before he composed it again. "He took an extra female into the Pride before his death. A Dunn."

"Holy shit," Torren said. "The child is half Dunn, half Tarian?"

"Yes," Rose murmured. "When Justin was killed in that war with the Blackwing Crew, the one that so angered you, Vyr, it was then that Callie, Brayden's mother, ran back to the Dunns. But they won't accept a half-Tarian cub, and she won't go rogue for him, so she left Brayden behind. She's asked us to find him a home."

"With a lion Pride?" Vyr asked. Oh, that was definitely hope in his eyes. He couldn't take his attention off the child.

"She doesn't have a preference. She just asked that he go to a mated pair who could protect him."

"A dragon and a polar bear would do," Nox said low.

Grim nodded once. "The Tarian Pride is in the middle of a shift in power. Half are trying to reestablish the lion council. Half are trying to put Ronin on the throne and rehabilitate the entire Pride. They're monsters. I'm sure I don't have to tell you that much."

Vyr clenched his teeth hard. "Why do you think my dragon wanted to put an end to them and claim their territory?"

"You lost them," Rose murmured. Her bottom lip quivered and she rubbed her cheeks, her blue eyes so round and full of emotion. "I can't imagine what that did to you or your dragon, or what the loss did to Riyah. I can't even imagine watching a person I love suffer like that. This would be taking in the cub of your enemy and raising him to be better than the

Pride he was in. It's an all-in kind of thing, Red Dragon."

Brayden was looking at Riyah's necklace, the locket her mother had given to her so long ago. She held out her hands, giving him the choice, and he took it. Growling little cub, he reached out and let her draw him against her chest.

Rose murmured, "He's been passed around so much, he's used to it. He hasn't formed a bond with anyone. He deserves to settle."

Vyr's voice broke on his words. "The Tarian Pride won't come back for him later?"

"If he goes to the half of the Pride who wants the council back in power, he will be raised to kill. That's his fate," Rose said in the saddest voice. "He's the son of a high-ranking Dunn lioness and the son of a Tarian Alpha. He will be raised like a weapon."

"Like you were," Vyr said softly to Grim.

"Yes, just like me."

Rose explained, "I'm the only female backing Ronin, and I don't have it in me to raise a baby. I love him, but he needs a mother and a father. Callie is ready to sign the paperwork. And if by some slim chance we win the Tarian War, we have all voted and support you taking the child and making him one of the Sons of Beasts. And if the council is revived and we lose this war..."

"The they'll have to rip him out from under the wings of the Red Dragon," Grim finished softly.

Riyah waited, holding back tears, hugging the child as he played with her necklace. He already felt so important. Already felt like hers. She'd seen him long before she'd known him. She'd seen him in Beaston's mind.

And now she could imagine the years ahead with Brayden, safe in their Crew, Vyr getting to be a father, the dragon having a chance to bond to offspring. To guide Brayden into being a good man instead of the weapon the Pride would turn him into.

Treasure, she whispered into Vyr's mind. *Choose this treasure. For me and the cub, but also for you. For Dane to grow up with. For Nox and Torren to love, for Candace and Nevada to covet and protect. Give the dragon the son I can't give him.*

"Can we do this?" he asked, his voice thick. "I mean...we don't have anything for him."

"Not true," Nox said. "I have the nursery in my closet still."

"Veto," Riyah said with a laugh. To Vyr she promised him, "We can figure everything out. Do you...?" She adjusted Brayden on her hip. "Do you want to hold him?"

Vyr's shoulders rose and fell as he stared at Brayden. And Brayden, brave little cub, he was holding the dragon's gaze.

Sparking silver reptilian eyes met curious bright green ones.

Vyr stepped forward carefully, slowly, eyes never leaving his. There was no sound. It was as if the entire Crew were holding its breath. As if the wind had frozen and the leaves didn't dare move on the trees. The birds were even silent. And when Vyr stopped shy of being able to reach the boy, Brayden released his grip on Riyah's shirt and held out his arms to the Red Dragon.

Vyr closed the gap between them and grabbed Brayden, cradled him close, and walked away. Just...left. He walked to the edge of the woods, and with his back to all of them, he fell to his knees. There was a deafening crack as the earth split in a jagged line leading away from Vyr. The air shook with the chest-rattling noise of Vyr's growl. No...not growl. As he rocked gently, side-to-side on his knees, it wasn't a growl that took up every air molecule in the clearing. It was a purr. It was a sound of satisfaction. Of happiness, if a dragon was capable of such.

And from here, Riyah could so easily see the little fists of the child go around Vyr's neck. Tiny, pale, clenched hands against a thick, tattooed neck. Tiny hands embracing a dragon. Accepting comfort from a dragon.

"C-can you feel that?" Nevada whispered as she stepped up beside Riyah and slipped her hand into hers.

Candace slipped her hand into Riyah's other one. "Can you feel the bond?"

Riyah closed her eyes, let the power of the dragon's humming take her over. She let her mind have the bond. It was glowing green and pulsing some beautiful color she couldn't even identify. She couldn't feel poison at all in it anymore. She searched for Vyr's darkness, but there was none.

When she opened her eyes, Vyr's shoulders were shaking, and she could hear the sniffles of her Crew beside her. Even Grim was wiping his eyes. The wind was whipping the trees all around, but she felt no breeze. Vyr had encompassed them all in a safe little bubble as his powers stormed through the woods.

And she could feel him. Her Vyr. There he was. His aura didn't pulse a muddy brown anymore, but a brilliant purple. His dragon had so desperately needed an anchor, and now he was holding him—the boy who wouldn't ever be the blood of his blood, but who could be the blood of his heart.

Come here, he whispered raggedly into Riyah's mind.

Come here. Just like he'd told the Sons of Beasts all those months ago in the shifter prison.

She squeezed Candace and Nevada's hands and released them. Tears streamed down her cheeks as she walked to her mate. The wind didn't touch her still as she sank down beside him and hugged his waist.

"We were supposed to get here, to this moment. To this little lion. Can you feel him, Riyah? Can you feel how strong he is already?" Vyr's voice was thick, and his eyes were closed as he hugged the boy with one arm and her with the other. "From the first time I knew you were mine, I always felt like there was something bigger, some bigger fate for us." Intense, emotion-filled silver eyes leveled her. "It's him."

"I can feel it," she murmured, pressing her face against his chest. She slipping her hand onto the child's back. "Little lion raised as the heart of the Red Dragon."

"He's ours," he said.

Riyah looked back behind them at Rose and Grim, and she nodded. *He's ours.* Grim dipped his chin once and smiled.

It wasn't just Brayden who was their fate. Vyr hadn't been able to keep away from Grim for a reason, one Riyah hadn't been able to figure out before now. Grim wasn't just a monster who matched Vyr. He'd had an important job all along. Everything happened for a reason.

Vyr had given Grim the mountains and a Last Chance Crew to take care of so Grim and his inner Reaper could steady out and be okay. Vyr had saved him.

And what had Grim done in return?

He'd saved Vyr right back.

Good Alphas.

And everything…*everything*…was going to be just fine.

Tarian Silver Lion

(New Tarian Pride, Book 1)

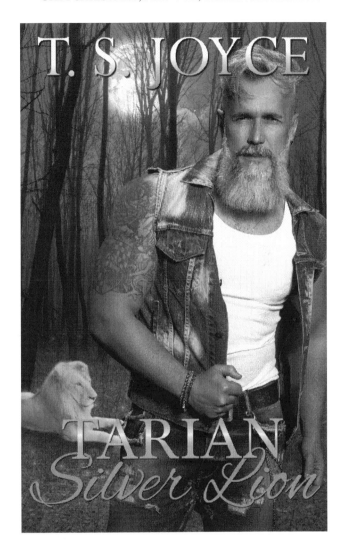

T. S. JOYCE

TARIAN

Silver Lion

PROLOGUE

"You're a good woman, Rose. I remember."

Rose jerked her attention to Talon Lawson's face. His eyes were open now and bright gold. He must've been in a lot of pain if his lion was still present. He had a thick silver beard and matching hair that was mussed just right. He was even more handsome than she remembered from his time in the Tarian Pride all those years ago. What was it? Fifteen years now? Something must've happened to his mate, Mariah. Mariah was a Tarian lioness, too, and wouldn't have allowed her mate to be beaten like this. She would've gotten him out of the Old Tarian Camp if she were still alive. Or she would've died trying.

"I'm not what you remember," she whispered as

she cleaned the long cut where one of his ribs had broken and stuck out of his skin. She'd wrapped the rib so it could heal properly, but this cut was still open and seeping. She was worried.

"If you aren't good, you wouldn't be wasting your time trying to save an old rogue like me."

Rose inhaled deeply and let the potency of his compliments wash through her. It had been a long time since a man was kind to her like this. But the timing was bad. His daughter had just traded her life for his. "The Old Tarian Pride has Emerald," she murmured low.

Talon's nostril's flared, and he grunted as he tried to sit up. His body was completely broken by whatever torture Cassius's Pride had done.

"Stop, stop, stop, you'll undo everything I've done," she said, frantically pushing his shoulders back onto the mattress.

He groaned in agony. His bare torso was a latticework of claw marks, bandages, and long, black bruises, as though they'd beaten him with a pole of some kind. He shouldn't have survived, but here he was. Steel man.

"I have to get her back," he said, his eyes wild.

Rose tried to smile reassuringly, but probably failed when she uttered the words, "Then let me be your claws." Why couldn't she hold his gaze? Because he was hurt? Because he'd gone through worse than her? Because she'd begun to care for him as he fought for his life? They'd become a little team without him knowing. She'd poured her energy into saving him so that she didn't have to think about her own time in Cassius's "care." Somewhere along the way, the unconscious man had started to matter to her. Terrifying, steel man.

He didn't understand. She could tell because he just lay there, staring at her, eyes so wide and confused, his hand gripping his stomach, his abs flexing with every struggled breath.

Rose might never see him again after tonight, so she did something she would've never ever done if she had the guarantee of a long life ahead. She leaned closer and pressed her lips to his forehead. And then she eased away and said, "Tonight, Ronin's going to war, and I'll be at his side."

"No," he rumbled in a deep, inhuman voice. He was going pale, and a cold sweat broke out across his skin. He would pass out soon. "No, Rose, I don't want you..."

"It's my choice. Emerald is important to Ronin, and Ronin is very important to me." *And you're important to me too, Talon.* "Your daughter is worth the war."

He was breathing so heavy, panting, through his mouth. His pupils were getting bigger, his eyelids heavy. Steel man, trying to stay awake. Nearly dead and still wanting to go back into Hell to retrieve his daughter. Steel Dad.

"You did so good," she whispered, cupping her hand on his cheek. His beard was soft under her touch. "You kept your girl safe all these years, but now you have to let us protect her while you rest—"

"Don't need rest," he gritted out, his voice breaking on the words.

Rose snarled and gripped his shoulders, looked him right in the eyes. "I'll bring her back. I swear it. No matter what, your daughter will come back to you."

His brows relaxed and his breathing steadied, and with his gold eyes going hazy, he said, "Be...my...claws."

It was in that moment of vulnerability when his

eyes rimmed with moisture. It was the moment he accepted he wouldn't be able to be a war-lion for his cub tonight...that look of deep regret that she understood so well...

That moment was the one that made her heart beat a little harder for Talon Lawson.

She scratched his beard gently and nodded. "I will."

And then his eyes closed, and his body went limp. She left the room, thinking she would never see him again.

And that was the terrifying part—the sadness in her chest at not seeing a man again. It wasn't her fate to pair up this late in her life. Her focus was to get the Tarian Pride rehabilitated with Ronin. That's all. That was everything.

No one understood how loyal her heart got when she chose a person. She never let go, never gave up on them. She couldn't afford to let her heart get attached to this one.

Caring for a man who was rogue and trained to run wasn't okay. Not for a lioness like her. He would leave, and she would hurt for the rest of her life.

If this war didn't kill her...falling for a rogue

would.

ONE

Talon Lawson had lost his anchor.

For the last two and a half decades, his entire world had revolved around his daughter, Emerald. But as he sat here, watching Emerald lean into her mate at the head of the sprawling dinner table, he knew he'd lost her.

Not in a bad way. He'd always wished for a pairing like this for her. She'd found a childhood crush. Or maybe fate had nudged them together. Ronin, Alpha of the New Tarian Pride, was a good man and caring toward his daughter. Protective of her just like every father dreamed for his child. A love match, like Talon had with Mariah, Emerald's mother.

His daughter was happy and stable and would

make an amazing queen for the Tarians. This Pride needed her kind heart and steel backbone.

No, he hadn't lost her in the tragic sense. He'd lost the need to take care of her. Or she'd lost the need for him to be her protector. Her hero.

She had figured out how to take care of herself, and now what? What was Talon's purpose?

Kannon, a dark-haired lion shifter next to him, leaned in and tinked his beer bottle against Talon's empty. "We're going into town later if you want to join us."

"Mmm? All of you? Why?"

"To celebrate."

Talon frowned. "Celebrate what?"

"Winning the war."

Talon huffed a laugh and shook his head. "Boy, you ain't won the war until every Old Tarian is snuffed out of existence. They're like a cancer. How many do you think survived last week?"

Kannon sighed and leaned back in his creaking chair, took a swig of his drink, a thoughtful look on Ronin and Emerald. "I counted nine of the Pride and four council members." He lowered his voice. "But all their females rebelled against them and traded to our side. One of their males, too, Orion." He twitched his head at a blond-haired bruiser who was sitting alone on the couch, watching football. "We have the numbers on our side now, and they've been shamed. Plus"—Kannon grinned—"we have a dragon."

Talon chuckled. "You do have that." There was no "we." Talon would leave as soon as he knew Emerald was settled. He wasn't here to crowd his newly-paired daughter. He just wanted to make sure she was adjusted to her new throne before he started his new life.

He wasn't very hungry tonight. Last week had just about done him in, and he wasn't quite healed yet. Apparently, being systematically beaten by a rival Pride and then dragged behind a snowmobile was bad for the health. He had good healing, thanks to his inner lion but, good God, those assholes had done a number on him.

He was a Lawson, though, and Lawsons didn't show weakness. Especially around a bunch of dominant strangers. Talon excused himself from the table and cleared his plate. The second he made it to the kitchen, a petite blond, Sora, reached out and tried to take the dish from him. "Sora," he rumbled, easing the plate out of her reach, "this isn't your old Pride. You don't have to do everyone's dishes." He twitched his head toward the table. "Go on in there and relax. Everything's okay."

She was looking at the ground, wringing her hands. She cast a glance at her brother, Orion, still sitting motionless on the couch, and then gave Talon a forced smile that looked more like a grimace. "I don't even know what that means anymore."

"You will," he promised, wishing he could revive all those Old Tarians who'd made her cower like this just so he could put them through a second death. Poor girl. If Emerald had been struggling to adjust this bad, it would've broken Talon's heart.

"You're safe with these guys," he murmured, sidestepping her to get to the sink. "And I'm wary of every shifter. Been on the run for years. These boys, though?" he said, looking over his shoulder at the table of chattering lion shifters. "They're different."

"Yeah," Sora said on a soft breath. Didn't sound much like she believed him, but this was her battle. Get tougher and learn to trust. Or stay a mouse her whole life. He hoped she didn't stay broken. He would talk to Emerald in the morning and tell her to pay special attention to Sora. Emerald was submissive, but tough as nails, and her care for people was unmatched. Probably Emerald had already noticed Sora was struggling. It's just the way his daughter was.

His phone vibrated in his back pocket. He dried his hands quick on a dishtowel and answered the call. "Yeah?"

"Hey, this is Wade at Effects Delivery. I'm towing your car and your belongings. I'm at the address you gave me, but some twat-wrinkle named Gray won't let me in the gate."

Aw shit, he should've given Ronin a heads up his things were being delivered today. "Hey, Ronin?" he called, covering the speaker of the phone.

Ronin was on his cell phone and leaned back in his chair, but looked back at Talon. "Your car?"

Talon nodded. "Yeah, I should've—"

"Nah, no worries. We have to be careful who we let in right now, though," he said, standing. "I'll head to the front gate with you."

"I can go to!" Emerald said. Sweet daughter.

"No, you two stay. Enjoy your dinner. It won't take me but a minute." Talon put his plate in the dishwasher and murmured into the phone, "I'll be right there," and then ended the call.

"You don't have to go alone, Dad," Emerald said, her dark eyebrows furrowed.

Before he could reply, the door opened, and in walked trouble. Holy shit, the woman who had nursed him back to health, Rose, was here. He'd waited to see her again for three days, but she didn't live with the Pride. He'd begun to think he would never see her again, but here she was, cheeks pink, straightened silver hair mussed from the wind, a blue sweater that made her pretty blue eyes pop like a spring sky.

"You look better," she said, her eyes wrinkling at the corners with her pretty smile.

Well, now, he was definitely not going to limp when he made his way to the coat rack by the door. Grabbing his thick winter jacket, he tipped his chin toward the door she was closing. "Want to go for a walk?"

"A walk? It's freezing out," Rose said, her delicately arched brows lowering over those pretty eyes of hers. She had this smile on her lips, though. One that said that she would still be up for questionable ideas.

God, there was something about her. She was tough, sweet, and happy, and all the things that drew in a man like him.

He tossed a look at Emerald who was smiling like a lunatic and waggling her eyebrows. "That one doesn't want me to go to the front gate alone. Apparently, I'm fragile now."

Rose snorted. "Fragile is not a word I would ever associate with you." She narrowed her eyes and studied him, then nodded once. "Okay, it's a date."

"Wait, a date?" he gulped out before he could stop his words.

"You should see your face right now. You look like I just proposed to you," Rose said, laughing as she made her way back outside. "You're driving."

Stunned by this little tornado and her directness, he murmured, "Oh. Okay," as he followed her out the front door and onto the porch.

It was cold as a witch's heart outside, and he shrugged into his jacket quick. His whole body still hurt, but he would be damned if he showed an ounce of pain in front of a Tarian lioness like Rose. She was tough as leather. Leather women didn't go for soft men. They went for men who were made of metal. That was *if* he was interested in her going for him. Which he wasn't. Because he was good at being a bachelor. And better off alone. And...stuff.

He'd thought she'd meant she was going to let him drive her car to the front gate, but nope. She'd meant a snowmobile. Fantastic.

"You know, the last time I rode one of these I was being dragged behind it," he muttered.

"It's important to get right back up on the horse," she said, tucking her whipping hair behind her ear. Gorgeous hair. Silver with darker gray streaks. Girls nowadays paid good money to have the silver look, and Rose had mastered it naturally. He bet it would feel great between his fingers. Oh good, he was turning into a creep now. Women like Rose were pure class. She didn't need some lowlife—"

"Shot of whiskey?" she asked, handing him a flask from the storage on the side of her snowmobile.

"Okay, I was just walking behind you, thinking about how classy you are, and you want to shoot whiskey. That's my kind of classy. Classy and badassy."

Tipping her pointed chin higher, Rose's eyes

sparked with amusement. "I've never been called those two words together before. I like it. You're a charmer, aren't you, Talon?"

Ooooh, he liked the way she said his name. She damn-near purred the word, and for the first time in a long time, he wanted to kiss a woman just to shock her. Or maybe to shock himself, he didn't know. Rose did something strange to his insides. She was like one of those heart defibrillator machines that shocked a man back to life. He'd been a damn corpse for years and, here he was, looking at this woman and taking his first breaths back in the land of the living.

But there were hard truths in his life.

One, he had nothing to offer a woman. He'd known Rose years ago when he'd lived in the Tarian Pride, and she'd been used to a well-kept lifestyle.

Two, he was an old grizzled rogue lion, grumpy sometimes and set in his ways, who had never been good with compromise or change, and women needed both.

Three, his insides were about as ugly as they could get right now. He'd gone through hell in that Old Tarian camp, and he didn't know how to talk about it, or to feel better. He didn't know how to make his lion less angry. No one could understand when he was this raw.

Four, he was leaving soon.

What right did he have to charm Rose? None at all.

So he offered his hand to help her onto the snowmobile. He had to push away the myriad of awful memories of being dragged behind one of these damned things. He swallowed his snarl and climbed on.

And as he started the engine and revved it, he said over the noise, "If I was a charmer at one time, I'm not anymore. I can't do dates, Rose."

"I know," she said, sliding her hands to his shoulders to hold on.

"Do you?"

"Why do you think I've stayed away?"

That part he hadn't understood. Still didn't. When he'd woken up here in the big house, his nightmare in the Old Tarian Camp done, Rose had been sitting on the edge of the bed. She'd looked so worried. She'd been ever vigilant, nursing him back to the land of the living. She hadn't left his side much for two days straight. He was hurt and couldn't do a lot of talking, but she hadn't seemed to need entertainment. She'd just changed his bandages, fussed over his healing, brought him food. Hell, she'd fed him when the bones in his hands were still shattered from fighting. And then after she'd gone to war with Ronin to rescue Emerald, she'd disappeared. "Why have you stayed away?"

She gripped his shoulders gently and said, "I know better than to fall for a man who is used to running."

And in this moment, he respected her even more. Not only was she beautiful and fearless and strong...but she was wise as well.

TWO

Truth be told, Rose had thought Talon would be long-gone by now. That's the only reason she'd come back to New Tarian Pride territory. She'd waited until she was sure he was headed back to his real life before she came to check up on the Pride. And really, she was lonely. Or her lioness was lonely. Talon had done something to her insides in the two days she'd taken care of him, and she didn't much like the hole he'd put into her chest when she wasn't around him.

You're a good woman, Rose. I remember.

Rose slid her arms around Talon's middle as they sped down the road on the snowmobile toward the front gate. She should've left her hands on his shoulders, which felt less intimate, but her stupid lioness was practically purring just being around him, and it had been so long since she'd been warm like this. The good warm. The kind that emanated from another person's body. She closed her eyes just to get lost in the feel of him. God, she was weak around this man. When he didn't shove her hands off, she smiled behind her whipping hair.

When the snowmobile slowed, she eased her eyes open and looked around his broad frame at the front gate. There was a one-man check-in stand, and Gray was standing in front of it, arms crossed as he glared at a man leaned up against an old black Chevelle with two white racing stripes down the front.

"Whose car is that?" Rose asked.

"It's mine," Talon said in that deep timbre of his.

Whatever she'd expected him to drive, it wasn't this. "But...when you lived here, you only drove old rusted-out pickup trucks."

The chuckle that rumbled through him warmed her to her soul.

"I was in that pickup truck phase for a long time. I got out of it about ten years back." He parked behind the check-in station and cut the engine to the snowmobile. "I bought an old rusted-out Chevelle instead and badgered Emerald into working on it with me every Sunday. Bribed her with dinner. It was our tradition."

Rose couldn't keep the smile from her face if she tried. "That's a lovely tradition."

Talon dismounted and gave her a wicked smirk, tilted his head toward the old muscle car, and offered her his hand. "Do you want to go for a ride in that old tradition?"

"Oh...well..." She shouldn't do this. She should ride her snowmobile right back to her cabin and get back to fixing the damage the Old Tarian did to it the night they'd kidnapped her, maybe drink a beer, watch her favorite Alaska shows, and hit the hay. Early. Because she definitely wouldn't be lying in bed, thinking about how it felt to have her arms around such a solid, burly man. Rose cleared her throat. "I can't just leave my snowmobile here. I have responsibilities and—"

"Gray, can you take Rose's snowmobile back up to the big house when your shift is over?"

Gray nodded and smiled big enough that Rose could see his dimples. Dangit. That was a yes, and when Gray waggled his eyebrows like he knew things about things, Rose traded her smile for a frown. There went her excuse. Now, how was she supposed to keep her heart safe from this…this…ramblin' man?

Talon was wearing a silly grin as he said, "Don't worry, Rose. It's not a date."

She swallowed a growl and stomped around the security bar that Gray hadn't lifted yet and directly to the passenger's side door of the very attractive vehicle. One yank on the door handle, and the driver enlightened her, "It's locked." She wanted to claw him. No shit, it was locked. Why was Talon still smiling like that? And Gray. Males were obnoxious. Rose lifted her chin higher and waited. Impatiently. They couldn't see her foot tapping, but she was sure she was beating a divot in the snow with the toe of her boot.

"Can you let the lady in while I sign the paperwork," Talon murmured. "I don't want her getting cold."

Driver Mc-driverson rolled his eyes and huffed a sigh like a brat teenager and crawled inside, popped the lock on her door, then scampered back out. Smart man. She really did feel about fourteen percent violent all of a sudden.

The car smelled like leather, oil, cleaner, and the piney wood-scented air freshener that hung from the rearview mirror. It was pristine inside. Rose touched the white leather stripe that ran down the driver's seat and now only felt about five percent violent as her inner lioness looked around Talon's den. Because that's what this was, right? He didn't put down roots, but he took care of his car. This was home for him. This and Emerald. Not a place.

Talon was talking low to the delivery man and Gray, signing some paperwork on a clipboard. She twisted in the seat and read the labels written on the boxes stacked in the back seat.

Kitchen.

Bedroom.

Memories.

Emerald's Baby Stuff.

A car and four boxes.

"Is this your whole life?" she asked Talon as he slid behind the wheel.

With a frown, he cast the boxes a quick glance and turned the key. The engine roared to life, the seat rumbling under her. Oh, hello.

"It's the important parts of my life. It made it easy

to pack up and go if I didn't attach to material things."

"Why did you do this, Talon?"

"Do what?" he asked, reversing the car past the tow truck the delivery man had unloaded the Chevelle from.

"Train yourself to live on the move."

She didn't miss the wince on his face as he threw the stick shift into first gear. He was still hurting. With a sigh as he hit the open road, he said, "Because I wanted to keep Mariah and Emerald safe. And being rogue isn't like what you think, Rose. There's not free territory out there that isn't claimed by some Crew or another. If we found some space, after a while, a Crew would move in and push us out or ask us to pledge. Or stalk us. You think the Tarians just let us go free when we ran from here? They're hunters who don't let anything or anyone go. They lost the family they could shit on the most when they had a bad day. The ones they could blame for any bad luck. You didn't have a submissive cub, Rose. And your grandson, Grim, sure as hell wasn't submissive either. I remember how you were. You and your mate. You were both tough as nails. We ran the night we thought Leon killed Ronin. He called that meeting and said they would be culling the submissives. I was a Tarian long enough to know what that meant, and I wasn't going to let them kill my daughter. Learning to live on the move? It was the easiest decision in the world. Tonight, I watched my daughter laughing and loving her mate, happy...safe...home. That's the life I dreamed of for her, but we had to wait for it to all work itself out."

Rose swallowed hard. "I feel like I should apologize."

"Apologize?" he asked, casting her a quick frown as he shifted gears.

"I..." Rose blew out a breath and tried again. "I made a snap judgement, but your life was completely different than I imagined. The judgmental old bitty in me thought less of you for running. For roaming. For keeping your mate and Emerald on the move all those years. But you didn't do it for selfish reasons, did you? You lived a harder life so that Emerald had a chance at surviving. And look what you did. Look where you got her." Rose relaxed back against the creaking leather seat and looked out the window, smiled at the man in the moon hanging low in the sky in front of them, illuminating the road ahead. "You're a good man and a good dad. Any wandering habits you picked up in all those years of moving...who am I to judge? Perhaps I should've made that same decision for Grim. Perhaps you were the one in the right. Perhaps I should've worked harder to save my grandson from being tormented into a monster in the Tarian Pride." She rolled her head against the seat and smiled at him, crossed her arms over her chest to ward of the cold. "Perhaps standing my ground made me the weak one and running made you the brave one."

"Hmmm," Talon murmured. "Or perhaps there was no right or wrong way. Perhaps we just had to make the decisions we thought were best at the time. I heard about your grandson. Sure, the council made the Reaper in him, but he's head of a Crew now and paired up with a love match. He came here to help Ronin get Emerald back. Him and his Crew. They're loyal to him, and he has a friend in the Red Dragon, too. He ain't doin' too bad, Rose. You did just fine with that one." His smile in the dim blue moonlight loosened the tight sensation that had constricted her chest. "When you get to our age, there is so much history behind us. So much story. And I don't know if it's the same for you, but I can lie awake every night and regret, overthink, and remember. And I have to pull myself back to the here and now because I'm not done yet." He tossed her a wink. "And you ain't either. Not even close, ya wildcat."

Rose snorted and barely resisted the urge to roll her eyes like the delivery driver had done. "Wildcat, huh? I eat boring fiber cereal for breakfast and take about a dozen vitamins and medications every morning. I get a senior citizen discount on movie tickets, and I'm getting arthritis in my hands so I can't do the things I used to and—"

"And you just went to war and whooped some dominant male lions' asses."

Shocked, Rose let her mouth plop open. "How did you...?"

"Oh, I asked around about you." He changed gears and gunned it on a straightaway.

The squeak that fell from Rose's lips was mortifying. She left her stomach clear back there on the road somewhere, and Talon wasn't slowing down. He hit another gear, and Rose clutched the seatbelt, prepared to bellow, "Good lord, let me live!" But right then, Talon let off the gas and the car slowed to a not-so-terrifying speed.

"Wildcats don't squeak," she said in a very small voice.

Talon chuckled and slipped his hand from the gearshift to her thigh. He squeezed it once and told her, "It was the cutest damn squeak I've ever heard."

"I'm a cougar," she blurted out.

Her cheeks felt like they lit on fire, so she pressed her cold palms there to cool the heat.

"Pretty sure you're a lioness. I saw you Change when I was here before, and unless you've been part of some gnarly experiments, I'm pretty sure you can't switch shifter animals right in the middle of your life."

"No...I mean..." Oh, God, how did she say this without further embarrassing herself? "You're young, Talon. And I'm..."

"I swear to God if you say 'old,' I'm going to pull this car over and make you walk back." He said it with a smile in his voice, but she dared a look at his face just to make sure his dark brown eyes were dancing. They were. "How old do you think I am?" he asked her.

"Don't tell me! I don't want to know."

Talon belted out a laugh. "Why not?"

He was teasing her, and enough was enough. She was embarrassed. Embarrassed! She didn't let men affect her like this. Never. She was above this and much too aloof to encourage his laughing at her.

"Turn here," she said, pointing at a mailbox. Or what would've been a mailbox if the Old Tarian Pride hadn't run it over with one of their ridiculous SUVs they'd souped up like they were preparing for the damn zombie apocalypse.

Talon slowed and turned onto the gravel driveway. "Is this where you live, or am I just turning around?"

"I'm up the road a ways. I can pick up my snowmobile tomorrow. I'm suddenly tired. You wouldn't understand because you aren't old."

Talon slammed on the brakes and jerked them to a stop. "Seriously, how old do you think I am?"

"Well, I had a child at fifteen, and my daughter was an apple that fell a little too close to the tree, if you know what I mean. She had Grim at sixteen, and Grim is a grown man. You have a daughter his age. So roughly fifty. And I know all about single fifty year old men in their mid-life crisis. They go for the young spring chickens and don't keep their interest on us mature ladies long."

"I'm not a mid-life crisis kind of man, and age isn't something I notice on a woman." He chuckled and said, "I sewed my wild oats much longer than you young breeders. I didn't have Emerald until I was in my thirties."

Hope blossomed in her chest. Honestly, part of the reason she'd stayed away the last few days was because she knew he was a runner, and part of it was because she'd assumed he was much younger, and she didn't want to feel gross for having a little schoolgirl crush on a younger man.

"I'm only five years younger than you," Talon murmured.

"Oh, thank God," she whispered, pressing her hand over her pounding heart. "I've been thinking how gross I am for having this...this...thing for a younger man, and—"

"You have a thing for me?"

"What? No. That's not what I said."

"Yes, it is. And I quote, 'How gross I am for having this thing for a younger man.'"

"Okay, okay! Okay." She held up her hands. "It's

not really a thing, per say. It was just the wrong word. That I used. I used the wrong word." *Oh hell, stop talking!*

"Even if I was fifteen years younger than you, I would still think you're a beautiful woman and I'd still want to take you out to dinner."

"Wait, what?"

"Dinner. Me and you. As cliché as it is, I truly feel like age is just a number."

"But your mate was younger than you. Mariah. I remember her. Why would you want to take *me* out?"

"I didn't pair up with Mariah because of her age, Rose. You're stuck on that part. I don't give a fuck about the number of years you've lived on this earth. I care about your experiences in that time. Besides, you're like wine, woman. You're even prettier now than I remember you back then. Your eyes are still just as blue, and you have the same wily smile. Your hair is a different color, pretty silver, and you wear it longer than you used to." He picked up a strand of her hair and rubbed it gently between his finger and thumb before he released it. "I like it this way. You look damn good to me."

He put the car in first gear and coasted up the

road toward her cabin while she sat there in utter shock at the butterflies battering her insides.

Sometimes a person could be complimented a hundred times by strangers or acquaintances, and it never really reached them. But then there would be that one person who could say a compliment, and it really went in the ear and settled in the mind. Talon was that person. Her cheeks were so warm right now, but she didn't cover them again. Instead, she slipped her hand into the crook of his arm and bit her bottom lip to hide the trembling smile there. "Thank you for all those kind words," she whispered.

"Been a long time?" he asked. This man knew a lot about a lot.

Rose cleared her throat and lifted her chin primly. "Maybe."

"So, is it a yes?"

"To dinner?"

"Mmm hmmm," he murmured, easing to a stop in front of her cabin.

Admittedly, Rose thought Talon was very handsome with his sexy-man smirk, dark eyes, and silver beard and hair that he'd obviously had taken care of at one of those modern barber shops. She'd noticed the tattoos on his big strong arms when she'd been taking care of him. And he smelled divine. Whatever cologne he wore was her new favorite scent. She loved a man who took care of himself. His smile was one of those that would bring a grown-ass woman to her knees. He was a flight risk, but in a way, that made this all a little more exciting. Yeah, it had been a while. A while since she'd felt anything for a man like this, a while since anyone had actually touched her heart with compliments, a while since a man had made her feel attractive. It was all a little addicting. And dangerous. But fun? And terrifying.

What was the harm in one little dinner? It was just two people eating food near each other. And talking. Just like they had been in this car. And that was probably okay. "When? I have a very busy schedule."

"Tomorrow. I'll pick you up in my hotrod. A hotrod for a hot granny."

"Oh, shut up," she said, swatting his arm while he cackled like a buffoon. She was trying not to laugh, but utterly failed.

He was cracking up so much, arms thrown around his middle, he ended up groaning in pain.

"Serves you right. You shouldn't laugh at a lady."

"I can't believe you had a hang-up about your age," Talon said, wiping the corners of his eyes.

"I don't see why my insecurities are something to laugh at."

"Because look at you!" Talon flipped down the sun visor, and there she was, looking grumpily back at herself in a tiny mirror. "Really, look at yourself, Rose. You were a stunner when I knew you before, and you're a stunner now. I know how old you are from before, but no one would ever guess your age. You know why?"

Rose swallowed hard and shook her head.

"Because you don't live like your age, do you? Tattooed forearm, ripped-up jeans, wild hair, leather boots, riding all over these mountains on your snowmobile. That saying 'you're only as old as you feel?' You're a great example, and you know it. There is nothing sexier than a woman in her prime who has the confidence of experience and the strength that comes with having to figure life out on her own. You are a woman who can handle your shit, Rose. Aren't you?"

Okay, now he could have a little smile. Clever

man. She nodded. "That I can."

"And there is that wicked glint to your eye and that sly-fox smile that's probably had half the men in these mountains tumbling over themselves to get your attention. But you don't give it easy, do you, Wildcat?"

"I'm picky and don't have time or patience for men's shenanigans," she conceded.

"Oh, I know. You're a fiercely independent woman who doesn't need a man for anything. The only way you would ever let yourself be with a male is if you *wanted* him there. He ain't needed. You would only throw attention at a man if he doesn't get in your way. If he empowers you. I'm gonna guess that those boys around here don't cut it, do they?"

"No. No, they do not."

The smile dipped from his full lips and then reappeared smaller as he searched her eyes. "Maybe try a man then."

Chills rippled up her forearms and, whooo, those butterflies got to flapping their wings in her stomach. How many years had it been since she'd gotten butterflies? She felt like she was in high school talking to her crush under the bleachers. This was ridiculous. She was being ridiculous. Everything was ridiculous.

"I'll go to dinner with you, Talon Lawson, on one condition."

"Name it."

"I pay for my own food."

He frowned. "Why?"

She offered him a Cheshire cat grin. "Because then it won't be a date." Rose pushed open the door, got out, and then shut it firmly before walking away. *Don't look back, be cool. Don't look back.*

"Hey, Rose?" Talon called.

His voice sounded off. Confused maybe, so she turned and asked, "Yes?"

His eyes had lightened and were locked on her destroyed cabin. "What happened to your house?"

Oh, dear. She hadn't thought about this part. She'd been so wrapped up in his charisma and conversation, she'd forgotten he hadn't seen the destruction. No one had but Kannon, who'd figured out she was missing in the first place.

Heart aching, she looked at her home and tried to see it from Talon's perspective. The front porch was gone completely, and there were two massive holes in the front wall. All the windows were busted out so she'd covered them in blue tarp while she was waiting on replacements to be shipped here. And her beautiful, precious rosebushes were all completely trampled or ripped from the ground entirely.

What could she say? How could she explain in as few words as possible that her house had been hurt, and it felt like her heart had been hurt right along with it? Simple honestly was always best. "You weren't alone."

"What do you mean?" Talon asked, opening his door.

As she watched him approach, Rose said, "You weren't the only one the Old Tarians took." She tried to smile because the ordeal was over and she could reassure him a little bit. That was kindness, not putting burdens on people who already carried so many of their own. "Cassius and four males from his Pride came for me in the night."

Eyes wide, Talon looked at her house. And when he dragged his gaze back to her, his eyes were a fiery gold and full of fury. All around them, the air grew heavier and heavier.

"Everything's okay. Ronin came for me. We didn't

know you were there in one of the prisoner cabins. We didn't know, Talon. If we had, we would've gotten you out of there the night Ronin came to rescue me."

"I saw the bruises," he murmured. "When I woke up, I was delirious with pain, but I remember the bruises on your cheek and neck. But the next time I woke up, they weren't there, so I thought I imagined them."

"I might not be a real wildcat, but I'm a pretty fast healer."

Talon inhaled deeply then released the breath, looking as troubled as a man could look. He pulled her close, hands on her waist, and then he shocked her completely with what he did next. He hugged her. Just...hugged. Just...wrapped his strong arms around her and stayed like that. Frozen, Rose didn't know what to do. She hadn't hugged a man like this in years. Didn't have any urge to. She was Rose, Tarian Lioness, badass, respected...untouchable. Or so she'd thought.

"I fought," she whispered.

"I know you did."

"I fought hard." Her guts felt like they were being torn in two.

Talon hugged her tighter. "I know."

Rose's lip quivered. Why did this embrace feel so good? She slid her arms around his waist and melted against him. As she squeezed her eyes closed, two tears streamed down her cheeks, and she pursed her lips hard to keep the sob trapped in her throat.

"Were you scared?" Talon asked.

Her voice would shake too bad if she spoke, and she couldn't bear that. So she nodded instead, her cheek pressed to his chest.

"Good," he said in a deep rumble. "You didn't shut down, you didn't go dormant, and now you're dealing with what happened. You're alive, Rose, because you're tough. Doesn't surprise me one bit that you were fighting them. That's the kind of woman you are. Beautiful badass."

His strong hand went to the back of her head, cupped it, and then stroked her scalp gently. It felt better than she could remember anything ever feeling before. Her lioness let off a soft purr, but she didn't try to stop it. Her walls were breaking. He'd taken a layer of bricks off with those three words. *Were you scared?* It was the way he'd said them that had shattered her defenses. He wasn't disgusted by the thought of fear. His voice had gone tender. He'd really wanted to know.

"Will you be able to sleep tonight?" he murmured.

She gripped his jacket in her clenched fists and nodded. "Eventually. I'm still in that strange phase where I think I hear something and check the house over and over until I'm exhausted and fall asleep on the couch with a shotgun on the coffee table near me."

"Shit," he whispered. "Rose, Rose, Rose. Why haven't you been staying with the Pride?"

"Stubbornness," she said with a half-laugh. "If I leave my home, it gives those men power. Most of them are dead now. I killed one of them in the war. They're ashes now, and I refuse to give power to ghosts."

Talon chuckled. "Atta girl."

There was a snarl to his voice, and he smelled like fur now. Fur and cologne—an attractive combination to her senses. Ugh, what a disaster she was. Crying and having a breakdown one moment, then sniffing Talon the next.

"I'm fine, really," she said. "My lioness will settle soon, and my defensive instincts won't be so kicked up. I'll get the house fixed up and get back to normal. You're just seeing me raw, when everything is still fresh."

"I like seeing you raw. I think you probably don't let the world see this side of you."

Rose eased back and released her grip on his jacket, then ran her fingernails from his short gray hair at his temple, down, down through his beard, massaging gently.

Talon rolled his eyes closed.

"Been a long time?" she asked, using his words.

His chuckle was deep and settled the heartache. "Maybe." He leaned down suddenly and kissed her forehead. It was fast, just a few moments of his soft lips lingering there, but it was powerful. Her lioness settled, her body relaxed, and she was filled with some sensation she couldn't identify. What was it, this steady feeling inside her?

"Go on, Wildcat," he murmured, swatting her on the ass. "Go on to bed, and no checking the house." He turned and pulled his jacket off, then tossed it in his car.

"What are you going to do?"

"I'll watch the house so you can get a good night

of sleep. I'd rather not be picking buckshot out of my ass by morning though, so leave the shotgun alone tonight, yeah?"

A stiff breeze could've knocked her over right now. He was going to watch the house? What did that even—?

Talon peeled off his black sweater and began shucking his pants. Oh good gracious, he was going to Change.

"Talon, you're still hurt," she said, gesturing to his bruised and mangled torso.

He just shrugged like it was nothing and kicked out of his boots. "I'll probably heal faster if I get a good Change in."

Naked. Talon was getting naked.

And, holy hell, that man had aged well. His muscles were rock hard and flexed with every movement, and she really shouldn't be staring, but her body was all tingly and her nipples had perked up like two little marbles. He had abs and tattoos. The butt...the butt was glorious. Had she ever liked a man's butt before? Possibly not, but Talon's butt was a work of art. The man hadn't skimped on his squats.

When he looked up, he had a smirk on his face

like he knew she'd been watching, but just didn't care. Rose wiped her damp cheeks real fast and cleared her throat. "I'll make you breakfast then. In the morning. As repayment."

Her piece said, she turned and marched to where the porch used to be. And then a little ungracefully, she climbed over the rubble and got her keys out, dropped them, found them again, shoved them into the lock, pushed open the door, and climbed inside on account of there not being stairs. She stood up, dusted off the knees of her jeans, and was about to tell him, 'You really don't have to do this,' but a massive silver lion was standing there, staring back at her with those glowing yellow eyes. His paws were the size of dinner plates. She didn't know if she'd ever seen a lion as big as him and such a light color. He was beautiful, if something so lethal could be called that. His mane was full, and he had lines of scars on his skin. His long tail twitched as he watched her. If they'd Changed together all those years ago when she'd known him, she couldn't remember his lion. And this one would be impossible to forget.

Her heart was pounding, but not from fear. It was pounding because, in this moment, she'd realized what that steady feeling was. The word clicked into place as he sat down, a guardian of her home for the night. A guardian of her.

Safe.

Tonight, she was safe.

And even if he moved on and left her behind, she would never forget what he was doing for her right now. He was giving her a gift. Sleep. He was allowing her to let her guard down and rest her weary mind and instincts for a little while.

He was a very, very good man.

Through a full heart and a grateful smile, she murmured, "I'm really glad you're back. Goodnight, Talon."

THREE

A wooden plank.

Rose had turned into a wooden plank. That's the only thing that explained the stiffness in her body. With a groan, she log-rolled over in bed and squinted at the harsh ray of sunlight that blasted her in the retina. What in the hades?

She reached out and yanked the alarm clock closer. 11:40 am.

Rose sat up in a rush. What sorcery was this? She only slept past six if she was lucky. She patted her body all over, but the stiffness wasn't from her injuries from the war. She lifted up the hem of her oversize T-shirt and looked at her stomach. Every claw mark and puncture wound from the war was completely healed, leaving only silver scars.

"Whaaat?" she whispered in shock. She pushed up her sleeve to expose the cut she'd gotten across the back of her arm the night she'd been kidnapped. It had happened when Cassius had slammed her against the full-length bathroom mirror. The cut had been to the bone and bad enough that she'd thought she would bleed out the first night she spent in captivity with the Old Tarian Pride. She'd said her goodbyes in her mind to Grim, Ronin, and the rest of the boys in the New Tarian Pride who were trying to change the fate of all lion shifters. To improve it. She was so proud of those boys.

That night had been hard, but now she was staring down at her arm at a silver scar. She was really okay.

There was a scuffling noise in the bathroom attached to her bedroom. She had been using the bathroom on the other side of the house since she'd returned from being taken. She hadn't been able to face what had happened in this one. Rose sniffed, scenting the air. The smell of cleaning solution and Talon's cologne wafted to her. Tenderly, she got out of bed and stretched her aching back. She hadn't in a million years ever imagined she would sleep good enough, deep enough, and long enough to get a stiff back like this again. Rose padded across the cold wood floors to the bathroom door opened just a crack. The light was on, casting a streak of gold across the floor and beckoning her closer.

With just a second of hesitation, she pressed her fingertips against the door and pushed. It creaked open until she could see him, Talon, on his hands and knees, scrubbing the floor. He wasn't wearing a shirt, and his powerful shoulder muscles flexed with every movement. There was a blue plastic bucket beside him half-full of water that had turned crimson.

Talon leaned back on his folded legs and jammed a finger at the broken mirror. "Tell me whoever did this is dead." When he looked at her, his eyes were glowing an impossibly bright gold color.

Rose crossed her arms over her stomach like a shield as she scanned the bathroom. He'd cleaned up the broken glass and all of the blood. He'd even hung the shower curtain back up, and the ruined bathmat was shoved into a trash bag on the ground. "Cassius did this. The girls killed him in the war."

Talon's broad shoulders lifted as he inhaled

deeply. He blew his breath out slowly, fists clenched on his thighs. "Rose, are you okay?"

She showed him the scar. "Yes, look. All healed. That good sleep benefited me."

"I don't mean physically, Rose. Are you okay?"

She swallowed hard. She wouldn't get away with a lie. Not when Talon seemed so attuned to her already. "I'm better now that I had a good night and you cleaned this room. I've been putting it off."

"Letting it haunt you."

Clever, clever man. She nodded.

He cast a quick glance at her toes and said, "Red is my favorite color. You look cute."

Cute? She was sixty-two years young, and yeah, shifters aged well, but she hadn't been called cute in a couple decades at least. Rose huffed a laugh and wiggled her toes. "Maybe I'll get my fingernails done the same color. For you. As a thank you for..." She shrugged and looked around. "For this."

"Yeah, well, I'm not done."

"What do you mean?"

"I mean, I can't leave here until this place is a safe home for you again."

The mention of him leaving felt like someone had

punched her right in the stomach. It sucked the air from her lungs, so she waited until she could draw a breath again before she forced a smile. "I'll be fine."

"Damn right, you will. I put in some orders for supplies. You gotta truck out back I'm gonna need to borrow to bring the supplies back here. I don't want to pay extra for shipping it. There's no point when I can do it myself. I made a list of stuff you need fixed up, Rose. It's a long one."

This man had stunned her on so many occasions since he'd come back, and here he was doing it again. "Oh, Talon, you don't have to do that. It's a lot of effort and—"

"I assume you aren't going through some human insurance company because you would have to explain how your house got destroyed like this, and from my time with the Tarian Pride, I remember the rules. No human law to govern us."

"I'm going to have to fix up the house in sections. I'm a retired florist. I get paid every couple of weeks from my retirement funds, but it mostly covers living expenses, not home repairs."

Talon snorted. "Woman, you aren't retired. I saw your greenhouse out back. You're a worker bee."

"Yeah, well, did you happen to see it's destroyed? They wanted to make sure Ronin noticed me missing. They wanted to get to him by taking the only female in his Pride."

Talon shrugged. "We will rebuild."

"How?" She frowned and leaned against the open doorframe. "How do you know what to do?"

Talon smiled. "The best job for staying on the move was construction. I got real good at finding teams that needed help for a week, a month, or two months. I learned a lot that way, too, didn't stay stagnant just hanging sheetrock or laying brick. I learned it all."

Oooh, he was a fixer. Okay, that was the sexiest thing in the world. She had a huge thing for men who were handy with tools. When her lioness purred, she covered it with a cough.

The smile that curved his lips was nothing shy of wicked, though, so she figured he probably heard it.

"I don't have the money to tackle it all at once."

"Let me worry about that. I've already been calling in favors on some of the supplies we need."

Stressed, Rose shook her head. "It still costs money, Talon."

"Have you told anyone in the Pride how you can't get your house fixed up?" he asked softly, hands relaxing against his jeans. His eyes were so direct and earnest on hers.

"No."

"I figured. You're tough, Rose, but you aren't alone."

Felt a little like she would be when he left, but she wasn't going to utter that little gem out loud.

"I got money just sitting in the bank getting moldy," he said through a grin. "No material possessions means I saved my earnings. If it bothers you, pay me back in time. But know that I'm not asking you to."

"Why are you doing this?" she asked.

Talon leaned toward her and tugged her hand until she stepped into the bathroom. He tugged and tugged until he eased her into his lap. "Because, Rose," he murmured against her hair, "you deserve to feel safe. You deserve to have something good happen to you. That's how the balance of the world works. You do good, and good comes back to you. There's gonna be bad patches in a life. What happened in this room was a bad patch. But woman, you can't have a rainbow without rain, right?"

Okay.

Okay, Rose.

Go ahead and fall a little harder.

He's catching you.

She slid her arms around his neck and nuzzled her cheek against his shoulder. How could affection feel this good? She hugged the boys and Emerald. She hugged Grim and his crew. But this was different. This was slipping into a warm, safe room where nothing could touch her, nothing could hurt her. She did have a lot of history, a lot of cracks in her story, but Talon was good at pointing to them and then wordlessly accepting them or fixing them without her even asking. He wasn't just a fixer of houses. He was a fixer of broken pieces.

"I will be sad when you leave," she admitted softly.

"You'll miss me?"

With a sigh, she nodded. "Something like that."

A deep chuckle reverberated through his body and drew a giggle from her. A giggle. Like a school girl again. She'd always believed in magic. She'd seen too much in this life not to. Talon made her believe in it even more. Magic was shaving years off of a person and, right now, sitting in a strong man's lap, growing a crush, she felt decades lift from her shoulders.

"All right," she said decidedly.

"All right, what?"

"Let's fix up the house together. And have fun while you're here. I'll pay you back a little at a time. Each month, you send me a postcard, and I'll send you a check. And that way I don't lose you all at once. I'll poke pins in a map for each place you send me a postcard so I can track where you travel. We can be pen pals."

"Pen pals, huh? I like it." He lifted her chin and searched her eyes. "You didn't answer me earlier. I won't ask again after this, but I need to know for certain. Are. You. Okay?"

Rose smiled then stretched up and pressed her lips against his. It would have to be answer enough for now.

She wasn't okay yet. Not completely.

But as he slipped his hand behind her neck and moved his mouth against hers, the world melted away, and she knew one thing for certain.

She would be.

FOUR

Like the bathroom, Rose needed to face everything that was done to her property. As she stood inside her greenhouse, amid all the shattered glass and her precious plants that had been hacked to pieces, her heart ached. This had been the place she'd found sanctuary when the loneliness made her feel empty. This greenhouse had been her sanctuary, and the Old Tarian Pride had shattered it just to hurt her. Most of the dead plants were dried floral carcasses on the ground or brown splintered twigs sticking out of toppled pots. This place wasn't her sanctuary anymore. It was a cemetery for old happy moments instead.

Talon had spent the morning hauling the

splintered wood of the destroyed porch to a burn pile in the side yard. It was freezing out, and she could hear his boots in the snow as he approached the greenhouse. She turned, not even trying to hide the hurt on her face through the open doorway. He strode straight for her through the snow with only old work gloves on, a black T-shirt, his silver hair mussed, and a worried look in his dark eyes.

Voice hoarse and thick, she said, "Nothing survived them."

"The Old Tarian Pride?" he asked, bumping his clenched fist on the splintered door frame. "That's not true, Rose. You survived and I survived. Emerald, Grim, Ronin, Kannon—"

"Okay, okay," she muttered with a sigh. He wasn't one to let her dwell.

Talon chuckled and patted her backside as he walked by.

Rose made a little squeak and clenched her butt cheeks in shock. "Did you just spank me?"

"Woman," he murmured, turning around and walking backward a few steps as he arched one dark eyebrow. "When I spank you, you'll know it."

Hells bells. Spanking was for young, wild people.

Not classy queens. Right? But as she watched Talon kneel down to right a trio of potted plants, the masculine curve of his butt pressing against his jeans, his triceps flexing with each movement, and his tattoos stark against his skin...she was a little curious.

"Hypothetically speaking, would a spanking hurt?" Oh, her cheeks were on fire! She didn't talk to men like this.

"It would sting, but it would feel so good you wouldn't mind."

"Oh," she said, wringing her hands. "So it wouldn't be punishment."

He threw her the naughtiest look she'd ever seen on a man's face. "Pleasure only."

"Hmmm," she squeaked out. "Interesting."

From where he knelt below her, his eyes sparked an intense gold. A hungry look washed over his face. "Leave a little pink handprint on that cute ass of yours. Remind you for a little while what I did to you. You're gonna want to look in the mirror at it so you can think dirty things. Think of how it felt when I was buried between your legs—"

When her phone rang in her hand, she startled so hard she dropped it. The dadburned thing clattered across the dirt floor and landed by Talon. With a wink that just about brought her to her knees, he handed her the phone.

Braindead, she answered the call without even checking the caller ID.

"Hey," Grim said. "Where you been, lady? I tried calling the landline, but you didn't pick up. Even called up at Ronin's, but they said you left your snowmobile there last night and they haven't seen you."

"Oh, I'm sorry. I'm here. At...home."

Talon slid his hand up the inside of her leg and asked where she wanted the pots stacked.

"Who's that?" Grim snarled.

"Wh-what?" Rose asked, trying to keep her mind on track. Talon's fingertips making their way to her inner thigh and his devilish smile were terribly distracting.

"I asked who's there with you? I heard a man's voice."

"Oh! It's Emerald's Dad. Talon. Lawson. He's helping me—"

"I'll be right there."

The phone clicked and went dead. Rose frowned

at the screen just to make sure but, yep, Grim had most assuredly hung up on her. Little protective toot. He'd always been like that. He wouldn't really show up, though. That meant taking a flight and leaving his Crew, and he'd only just gotten back home after the Tarian War.

Silly grandson.

Rose texted him quickly just to make sure he wasn't online, looking at flights. *I'm fine, boy. At home having a nice time with a nice man. I'll call you later. Tell Ash hello for me. I miss you all very much.*

Crisis averted, she set the phone on the edge of a table and smiled down at Talon who was still exploring her with his touch. She ran her hands through his hair, nails against his scalp, and couldn't, for the life of her, tell if he was growling or purring. The sound he made sure got her blood pumping, though.

Her legs trembled as he wrapped her inner thigh in his strong hand, and when he leaned forward and set his teeth gently to the sensitive spot right over her knee, she gasped. She was wearing leggings and could feel every point of his teeth. With a soft moan, she leaned forward and gripped his hair for balance.

He adjusted to his knees and slid his hands to the backs of her legs, laid his teeth on her a little higher, a little harder.

Rose swayed into him and rolled her head back. Everything had been heavy for so long, but right now, he was cutting the weight from her with every nip. He'd started a fire in her, and he was tending it as he clamped his teeth higher, right at the apex between her legs.

The world didn't exist anymore. Nothing did except for Talon.

Go ahead and fall.

He ran his hands up the sides of her legs, then under her sweater and gripped her waist. She hadn't been touched like this in so long, but did her age mean she didn't *deserve* to feel adored? To feel coveted? To feel beautiful? She didn't think so.

Talon was purring against her skin, and her breaths came in quick pants as his fingertips trailed warmth up her back to her bra. He unsnapped it in one easy movement, then dragged his palms under the material across her ribs until he cupped her breasts.

"Talon," she whispered helplessly. She rested her

hands on his broad shoulders for balance and leaned into his touch. The feel of skin on skin held such power. She didn't understand why. Perhaps it was because it had been so long since she'd felt cared for like this, or maybe it was just Talon and whatever charisma he and his lion possessed. Sweet addiction. That's what this was. She would do awful things to never have this end. To fuse his hands to her, to cement this feeling to her soul. The one of belonging to someone. Of being possessed by them.

Of not being alone.

For once…not being alone.

He pushed her sweater up and kissed her stomach. And God, his beard felt divine against her skin. She was totally lost already. He dragged his fingers down her sides as he kissed her stomach, just a hint of tongue against her skin. Down, down, his hands went until his fingers hooked in the elastic of her leggings and dragged the material right down with him. It was so smooth, there was no time for her to balk or overthink or let her insecurities have her head. Three downward trailing kisses, and his mouth was on her sex.

It's okay to fall.

His steel hands eased her back against the edge of the table, and his tongue lapped at her clit. She let off a long moan.

"Louder," he snarled. "Tell me how much you like it." And then he splayed her knees farther apart and slid his tongue inside her.

Rose cried out his name, over and over as he stroked into her until she was right there. He was growling loudly, the sound vibrating the air around her, pulsing right through her, consuming her. It was a feral sound of pleasure. She was doing that to him, just by enjoying herself. Having power like that over a man like Talon was the most erotic thing she'd ever been a part of.

With a snarl, Talon yanked her leggings to her ankles, ripped them off the second she lifted her feet for him, and then he stood, threw them to the floor. He spun her around, and all Rose could do to stay upright was splay her hands on the table.

Talon cupped her sex as he rolled his hips against her ass, and his erection was so hard it pressed against her through his jeans.

Right as she found the rhythm of them moving together, him rubbing against her, he pushed two fingers into her deep. "Oooooh," she moaned, tossing her head back.

Talon rumbled, "Good girl," and clamped his teeth onto her sensitive earlobe.

And then the sting of that slap on her bare backside came shockingly fast. It was a sharp pain and then direct pleasure as he stroked his fingers into her and then rolled against her again, that sexy snarl rattling from his chest to her back.

The sound of his zipper just about did her in.

Ooooh, she liked spankings. In desperation, Rose spun around and tugged his shirt over his head, and then she was shoving his pants down his muscular hips with fumbling fingers. His long, thick, swollen cock was freed from his briefs, but she only got a glimpse of it before he took it in hand and guided it to her slit. Rose cried out as the head of it slid inside of her. Legs splayed, the table behind her creaked as it slid a few inches back and rested against the wall. Thank God, because she needed the support as he pushed into her again, hard.

Fuck. Fuck! Nothing could touch this feeling. "Deeper," she begged.

Flexing his hips, Talon pushed into her farther. He

gripped her waist and held her in place as he stroked a little deeper into her each time.

Rose didn't even know what the hell she was yelling anymore. All she knew was that the tingling, erotic sensation between her legs was building at a blinding pace, and she wanted more. She wanted it all.

Powerful Talon, the man rammed into her and hit her clit as he filled her, and all Rose could do was sink her nails into his back and hold on. Over and over, he pumped into her until she saw stars at the edge of her vision. Her orgasm came so intensely she dragged her nails down his back.

He let off a bellowing roar as he drove into her hard...and then hesitated. Her body was pulsing fast, but she didn't miss the deep throbbing of Talon's dick inside of her. The grunts that he made as he jerked into her, emptying his seed, were so sexy. Her release fluttered on and on, slowing and then easing as he continued to move inside of her.

Gasping for breath, Rose rested her forehead on Talon's and closed her eyes, cupped his cheeks with her hands. Soft beard under the pads of her thumbs, strong chest against her soft one. His lips finding hers as he remained buried deep inside, connecting them both. He'd just changed the way she felt about herself, about life, about everything with the simple power of touch.

A long-buried part of her perked up and grinned. *I've still got it.*

She wished she was poetic, or good with explaining how much something like this meant to her, but that wasn't Rose. Pretty words and thoughtful sentiments belonged to her when she was younger, but she'd lost them a long time ago.

Now, she had that say-it-how-it-is syndrome.

"Well," she murmured, "that was pretty fuckin' athletic."

There was a second of silence, and then Talon belted out a single, echoing laugh.

Rose snorted and then let off a giggle.

And then Talon was chuckling.

Rose hugged him tight as she lost it completely and cracked up. Then there was Talon, filling the entire greenhouse with a baritone laugh that made her heart happy.

And as they wiped tears from the corners of their eyes and petted each other, lost in a passionate moment that had turned to fun, she found herself grateful.

Rose had never felt more alive, but it was more than that. As she looked around the greenhouse, all of the damage didn't seem as important anymore. It wasn't so dire. The hurt wasn't everything. In fact, right now, it counted for very little.

She'd thought this place could never be a sanctuary again, but Talon had fixed that little broken part of her. He'd come in here and made this place mean something again.

And as he turned her slightly and looked at her rump with a smirk on his face, she broke into giggles again. He'd left a perfect pink handprint.

A greedy little part of her lioness wished it would never go away. "We took back the greenhouse," she murmured breathlessly.

Talon's dark, dancing eyes looking right into her soul made her heart thump wildly. "We sure did, Wildcat."

****

You're with Rose, aren't you?

Talon read the text from Emerald twice. How should he tackle this one. He'd been sending her the

293

'I'm fine' texts for two days while he'd stayed with Rose, but Emerald worried. She cared about people deeply, and was sensitive, like her mother had been. She'd been asking over the past year if he would ever date again, but he didn't want to get her hopes up with this.

Run.

The lion was a relentless asshole lately. The smell of coffee permeated the house, and Talon sat up and rubbed his hands down his beard. It was barely dawn, and hard to see in the dim room.

It was one of those happy scenes from a movie, where he should be lying here all happy and content, but...

Run. We've been here too long.

His phone screen lit up again. *Dad, you are many things. A protective, shit-handling, intimidating, loyal old fart. But you aren't an avoider. Are you having trouble dealing with what happened when you were with the Old Tarian Pride? We've always been able to talk, but you've shut down about what happened there. I would call, but I'm pretty sure you're with Rose, and I don't want to wake her.*

He sighed, kicked the bedsheets off his legs, and

rubbed his aching ribs for a few seconds before he responded. *I'm helping her fix up her house. I'm alright. Stop worrying. And I'm not an old fart. I'm a very young fart. Dad.* Send.

*OMG why do you always sign your texts with Dad? I know who I'm messaging. *laughing face emoji**

Talon snorted. Little turd. He would now sign every text with 'Dad' because he could just imagine her laughing to herself. And his daughter deserved laughter after everything she'd been through.

This bed sure felt empty without Rose.

Run.

She'd gotten up early today, and he'd made love to her slowly. And after, she'd snuggled against his chest for a while, her freezing cold feet warming between his calves, and then she'd said she wanted to make him coffee. Sweet Rose. How had he gotten so lucky with her?

Run. It's not lucky. She's getting you addicted to this place. To this feeling of belonging, but we don't belong.

Talon's attention darted to the window for the tenth time since Rose had wrapped herself in the comforter and padded out of the bedroom. Bad news.

That's what roamers did. They started looking out windows and imagining the places they would go next. They started feeling trapped.

Run.

With a growl, Talon pushed out of bed and ran his hands through his hair roughly. Sometimes he wished he wasn't a shifter at all. He and the lion didn't always see eye-to-eye.

But from here, he could see the broken mirror through the open doorway to the bathroom, and a long, low growl rattled his throat. And it was times like these that he did appreciate the lion. Because as long as he was here, no one would ever hurt Rose again.

He looked out the window again and winced, shook his head. Why couldn't he just appreciate this place for what it was? A safe haven with a woman he wanted to spend the rest of his years learning about. She had a million layers, and each one she revealed was more consuming than the last.

Talon pulled on a pair of sweats and followed the scent of fragrant coffee down the hall and into the living room. Rose wasn't in the kitchen like he'd expected. When he saw her standing with her back to him, the comforter draped loosely around her shoulders, he drew right up and froze in awe. She leaned on the open front doorframe, her silver hair cascading down her shoulders, her face slightly turned and catching those first gray streaks of dawn on her high cheekbones. She said things sometimes that made him shake his head and chuckle because it was so apparent that she didn't know how damn beautiful she was. Her eyes crinkled at the corners from years of smiling, and her skin had lost some of its firmness, but was replaced with a softness he couldn't stop touching. Her tattoo ink, like his own, had lost the crisp lines over time, and now they had more character. He could see her shoulder bones as she stood there stoically, soaking up the dawn, a mug of steaming coffee cupped in her hands.

Sometimes Rose called herself old, but that wasn't right at all.

Her years were one of the most attractive things about her.

She was broken in just perfectly.

Unable to stand this far away from her, Talon walked up behind Rose and slid his hands up the soft skin of her back. He wrapped his arms across her chest in a silent promise to protect her as long as he was here. To be at her back until the moment they were separated. He rested his cheek against the side of her head and smiled when she melted back against him. And he stood here and watched the sunrise with her. No words were needed between him and Rose, but he had a favor to ask of his lion because for the first time in a long time, he wanted to belong somewhere. He wanted to belong to someone. He would give anything to belong to Rose, and to moments like these.

Let me keep her. Let me stay.

FIVE

"I need to get groceries," Rose said over the Queen song blaring on Talon's radio.

"You mean you need sustenance after all the horizontal exercise we've been doing?" he asked cheekily.

"Don't be crass," Rose said through a private smile as she held her hand out the open window of his Chevelle and caught the wind against her fingertips. It was still cold, but the sun was out, and she hadn't stuck her hand out a window in ages. "But yes, I need sustenance."

Talon chuckled and took a right onto New Tarian Pride territory. At the security station, it was Kannon's shift right now, and he froze mid-bite of his burger and frowned at them.

Talon pulled up to the window and told him, "We need to pick up Rose's snowmobile. Do you know where Gray parked it?"

Kannon was staring at Rose with an odd and unreadable expression on his face. He took a slow bite of his burger and chewed it like a cow chewing its cud.

"Cat got your tongue?" Talon asked him, his arm resting on the open window.

"No," Kannon drawled. "But I'm pretty sure that cat has yours." He pointed to Rose.

Utterly stunned, she didn't even get a word out before Talon was driving them through the gate Kannon had buzzed open.

"Do you think he can tell that we're...we're..."

"Fucking like rabbits?" Talon asked.

"No! Together!"

Talon ran his hand down his beard and smirked. "Probably. We are giving off that sexy pen pal vibe."

Oh. Rose's heart dipped to the fragrant leather seats. She'd had so much fun and been so distracted the last couple of days with Talon, she'd forgotten about the pen pal deal. Forgotten he was leaving at all.

Now a selfish part of her wished the house would never be repaired so he would stay.

She was prepared to pout, but he reached over and wrapped his hand around hers, settling the upset emotions that were building like a storm in her chest. "We aren't there yet," he murmured. "Don't start counting down."

"Oh, you're a mind reader now?"

He threw her a sideways glance and hit the gas, spinning out on the gravel road.

Rose laughed and swatted his arm. "You can't get out of every serious conversation with a gas pedal."

"I know that. I have other weapons, too."

"Like?"

Talon waggled his eyebrows, and now Rose was snickering again. "Ridiculous man."

But she forgave him and slid her hand to the inside of his elbow, her favorite place to rest it while he was driving the stick shift. He patted her hand there and then rested his palm over her knuckles as he pulled to a stop in front of the big cabin.

Everything was different. It was like the colors were brighter. Maybe it was just the sunny day that was making everything so brilliant. There were little green grass shoots poking through the melting snow. A bird in the tree nearest them had feathers on his chest the same color as the sun, singing a pretty little song that made her happy down to her soul, and even the stain on the cabin looked new. More orange than she remembered.

Ronin and Emerald were sitting on the porch stairs of the cabin. Ronin was tying his work boots and Emerald was wrapped in a blanket, cupping a mug of something hot and steamy in her hands.

"Hey, Dad," she called with a wave. "What are you doing out so early?"

Talon eased to a stop and pushed his sunglasses to his silver hair. "Bringing this one back to pick up her snowmobile."

He was so handsome that sometimes it was hard to look away from him. "I like to stare and I don't care," she sang under her breath.

Talon looked over at her with a smile. "Poetic," he complimented her.

"I'm using all of my wiles to keep you attracted to me."

He slid his hand over her thigh and squeezed.

Under his breath, he said, "Make me any more attracted to you, and we'll never leave your house again."

Mmmmm, yummy man. Her cheeks had to have been positively pink with pleasure. She wiggled her shoulders and hips in a little happy dance with the music.

When Talon shoved open the door, he pointed to her and demanded, "No moving. I'll get your door."

One of those songs that Grim used to sing came into her head. *What a man, what a man, what a man, what a mighty good maaaaaan, what a mighty mighty good maaaaaaan...*

Talon jogged around the front of the car and opened her door for her, then helped her out. It wasn't like she needed it. She was a Tarian lioness after all. She didn't need help with anything...but it was really nice and sweet that he was a gentleman with her. Well, outside of the bedroom. He was an utter rogue inside of it.

She followed right behind him, staring at that fine butt of his flexing with every step. She wanted to bite it. A growl rattled up her throat and Talon, that fine man, gave her a wicked glance over his shoulder.

When she looked up at Emerald and Ronin, she skidded to a stop beside Talon.

The two of them were sitting there frozen with matching what-the-fuck looks on their faces. Ronin held two shoestrings in his hands that were only halfway laced up his work boot. And the only thing that moved on Emerald was the steam of her drink.

"You two seem...different," Ronin drawled out.

Rose cleared her throat and straightened her spine, lifted her chin. "It's a beautiful day out. I'm in a good mood."

Emerald's bright green eyes narrowed to slits. "What happened to your hair?"

"My hair?" Rose patted it. Oh, God, there were leaves in it and the right side was like a bird's nest. Right before they'd gotten into the car, Talon had made love to her from behind in the woods after they'd Changed together. Mortified, Rose frantically plucked foliage from her tresses and tried to comb it through with her fingers.

Talon wasn't even hiding his laughter. "Here, let me help. There's a stick in it."

"Why didn't you tell me I look like a mess?" she whispered.

"Because you don't. You look like a well-fucked, sexy—"

"Shhh!" she hissed, swatting his hand away.

Incorrigible man was smiling so big, and everyone was going to know she was a hussy for him.

Finding the very last single shred of her dignity, Rose stood as tall as she could, lifted her chin, shook out her wild hair, and walked proudly past Talon toward her snowmobile.

Talon smacked her ass.

With a yelp, Rose's gait hitched, and then she went back to walking. Like royalty.

Talon snorted behind her.

"What am I even supposed to do with this?" Ronin asked. "The only reason Grim is not here right now is because I told his panicked ass that he was mistaken, and that his *grandmother* did *not* have a boyfriend. Or…manfriend?" He muttered a curse under his breath and tried again. "Bedmate?"

Rose was perfectly fine letting him continue. He sounded so uncomfortable with this discussion. This was kind of amazing.

"Oh, my God, Ronin," Emerald said, her mouth agape as she stared up at her mate. "That's my dad.

Don't say bedmate."

"I don't know if I'm okay with this," Ronin called from behind Rose. "You're my...and he's Emerald's..."

Rose mounted the snowmobile and glared at Ronin. "I'm old, not dead."

"You're not old," Emerald argued.

Talon had stayed by the car and was leaning against the front of it now, watching them with a remorseless smirk on his lips, as though he didn't give a single care about everyone's discomfort. Okay, now Rose was biting back a smile.

"Yeah," Rose said. "Emerald is right. I'm not old. I don't feel old. I feel like me. Just Rose. And I can have a crush—"

"Grim would literally shit himself if he heard you say the word 'crush'—"

"Ronin Dillon Alder, if you and Grim have it in your heads that I don't deserve happy moments with a man, you are dead-ass wrong."

"Oh?" Ronin said louder. "Am I *dead-ass* wrong, Rose?" His eyes turned gold as he took three steps closer. "You're *my* grandma to protect!"

"Or cock block?" Rose asked. "You realize I'm much more than just someone's grandmother, don't you? I'm a woman, too. I have feelings and all that shit. I don't want to shock you, but I can still be attracted to a man. That part doesn't just die when I hit grandma status." She enjoyed the stunned, angry look on his face. His mouth was hanging open, hahaha.

"Don't say cock block!" he ordered.

"Cock," Rose said.

"Block," Talon finished for her.

Rose snorted and tried to swallow down her laughter. Ronin's face was getting so red.

Static blasted across the walkie-talkie at his hip, and Kannon said, "Hey Ronin."

Ronin ignored him. "But you're—you're—you're Rose. You're strong and independent. You already had your mate—"

"Hey Bonin' Ronin," Kannon said, an annoying smile in his voice.

Ronin snatched the walkie-talkie from its sling, pushed the button, and snarled, "Don't call me that."

Okay, this was a little funny. Made more so by Talon's shoulder-shaking silent laughter behind Ronin. And now Emerald was snickering, too.

"None of this is funny," Ronin pointed out,

rounding on them.

"Hey, Alpha," Kannon said.

"What?" he bellowed loud enough for Kannon to hear him all the way at the check-in station.

"Rose is bangin' Talon, boink, boink."

The Alpha of the New Tarian Pride just stood there, face lookin' like a cherry. Emerald jogged over and slid her hands up his back. "Babe, I love that you're protective over Rose, but she's not doing anything wrong. She likes a man. So what? I called this happening the night of the war. Rose fixed him up, and there was something in her smile when she left the room. She looked...happy." Emerald nodded to Rose. "It's good to see you happy, and even better for me to see my dad happy. So whatever you two are doing...keep it up. You deserve the smiles on your faces." She tugged Ronin's arm. "Come on, ya crazy. We have to get the girls into town."

"Did you hear me?" Kannon asked over the walkie-talkie.

Ronin turned and made to throw the handheld radio at the side of the cabin, but stopped himself mid-throw. Jaw clenched with anger, he pulled the contraption to his lips and jammed his thumb on the button. "Fuck off." And then he turned the volume down and slammed it back into the sling at his hip. And then he kicked at the snow.

Today was the best day ever.

"Why are you taking the girls into town?" Talon asked, pushing off his car. "Are they okay?"

"Oh, yeah, they're fine," Emerald said. "A couple of them have decided to find different Prides just so they can distance themselves from the Tarian Pride and what they went through, but Annamora and Sora and Maris are staying for sure, and they want jobs. And honestly, I think it would be good for them. Give them some confidence. We couldn't find any job openings online, but I figured if we went into town, they could fill out some applications and hope a spot opens up eventually."

Well, Rose perked up at that. "I think that's a great idea," she murmured. "Those women are tough, but they had their confidence shaken in that awful Pride. Let's help them get their legs back under them."

Emerald looked relieved and exhaled a big breath. "Okay, thank goodness. I was afraid I was pushing them too hard, too fast."

"No, give them something to focus on. Remind them that it's okay to care of themselves for once." She'd been struggling with similar feelings before Talon came along. Self care was important for a woman.

"Do you…" Emerald cleared her throat. "Do you maybe want to come with us? We can do a girls' day. Maybe do dinner afterward."

Rose's whole face stretched with a smile. "I would love that."

"You ladies want to take the Chevelle?" Talon asked.

"Whoa!" Emerald exclaimed. "You would let us drive your hotrod for the day?"

Talon gave Rose a wink. "It's the perfect girls' day ride. I need to pick up supplies, so I'll borrow a rig from one of the boys here and get a work day done."

"Supplies for Rose's house?" Ronin asked thoughtfully.

"Yeah, it's a mess. That Old Tarian Pride did a number on it."

"I got a full-size truck," Ronin said. "Do you need help?"

"Are you asking so you can grill me the whole

way to the lumber yard?"

Ronin shrugged. "Maybe."

Talon scratched the corner of his mouth with his thumb and chuckled. "Fair enough."

Plans all changed up, Rose dismounted the snowmobile and made her way to Talon. She leaned into him and murmured, "I'm gonna kind of miss you."

"Kind of?" He offered her a crooked smile and leaned against the car again, arms crossed over his chest. "Say what you mean, Wildcat."

Rose rolled her eyes heavenward and cocked her head at him. "I'm going to miss you today."

He kissed her quick, just a peck, and patted her backside. "I'm just guessing, but it must've been very hard to be the only female in this pride for a while."

Oh, Talon was very intuitive. It was one of the things she loved about him. *Loved about him.* Oh, no, she needed to be careful with that. Those were big feelings. Scary feelings. Feelings she didn't have a right to have for a man who was upfront with his desire to leave soon.

Missing him today would be a little taste of how the rest of her life would be.

Rose was careful to keep her poker face because she wasn't one to show weakness, but inside, it felt like a hole had been torn into her heart.

Talon's dark gray brows drew down, and he brushed the knuckle of his finger down her cheek. "Where did you just go?"

Rose forced a smile and took the keys from his other hand. "Nowhere. I'm still here."

And here was where she would always stay.

The thought that this was home used to make her feel steady and comfortable, but now everything was different.

When he left, the colors around her wouldn't be as brilliant anymore, and there would be less to look forward to. Less laughing, less letting her guard down, less feeling safe, less exposing her soul and knowing she was accepted.

Less everything.

When he left, home was going to feel very empty.

SIX

"Are you staying?" Ronin asked. Direct and to the point. Talon actually liked that about him, but he didn't like answering direct questions he wasn't ready to answer yet.

"I've never been much of a stay-er," Talon murmured, staring out the window as the town of Telluride blurred by. "I was with the Tarian Pride my whole life until the day we thought Leon killed you and he was talking about culling the submissives. I was looking down at my daughter, scared for the first time ever, scared they were going to hurt her and I wouldn't be able to do anything. That I was going to fail her as a father. Someday, you and Emerald will have cubs of your own, and you'll realize that for all the excitement and fun and good, there are also moments that terrify you."

"When we have cubs, Emerald will want you around, you know," Ronin said, not taking his eyes off the road. "I want you to pledge to me. To the New Tarian Pride. I want you to be a part of this."

The lion inside of him snarled at the thought of being caged into a Pride, and Talon owed it to Ronin to try to explain. He swallowed hard so the noise in his throat would stop. "Do you know what happens to a lion when you make him roam? Or to a lioness?"

"They always have to roam?" Ronin guessed.

"Not always, but most of the time. Emerald is settling well. I can tell. Her eyes aren't darting to the road, she isn't twitchy, she isn't looking out the window all the time, feeling trapped. She isn't pressing the outskirts of the territory when she Changes. I've been watching for any of the signs Mariah used to get, and she just doesn't have them."

"I remember your mate from when I was a kid. What happened to her?"

"Car accident. The first year was absolute hell. I had Emerald, though. We moved eight times that year."

"Jesus," Ronin whispered.

"It's addictive. When we got settled into one place, other shifters would threaten us, or something would spook Emerald, or we would get sad about her mother and want something else to focus on."

"And roaming took that focus?"

"At first, moving was necessary to escape the Old Tarian Pride, but eventually, I guess it was our coping mechanism for dealing with life."

"So break the habit."

Talon huffed a dark laugh. "I wish I could, but it's not up to me."

"Who is it up to?"

Talon blinked slow and let Ronin see the lion in his eyes. He knew they'd be gold. Talking about the cage of a Pride constricted his chest and made the cab of this pickup feel too small.

"You like Rose," Ronin said, "so you should know how it is for her. You should know what you'll do to her when you leave."

Talon didn't even try to hide his growling now. "Ronin, I like you, but you don't have a say in what Rose and I do or don't do."

"She doesn't attach to people, Talon. She is sooo

careful. So careful." He pulled into the gravel parking lot of the lumber yard and parked right up front. "Her kid was a piece of shit. Never appreciated her or Byron, her mate. Dumped Grim on her right when she lost Byron and then left. Was manipulative and only came back when she wanted money. And if Rose didn't help, she would threaten to take Grim and never let Rose see him again. And he was the only steady thing she had left by then. Imagine that, Talon. How it was for her. You remember how awful the Tarian Pride was? Rose isn't submissive by our standards, but by the council's? She was nothing, treated like a pariah. Were you there the day Grim turned into the Reaper?"

"Fuck," Talon murmured, squeezing his eyes closed at the awful memory. He'd been lucky enough to forget it until now.

He pressed the heels of his hands against his eyes as he saw her face in his mind. Rose had watched Grim in a dominance battle. Watched him and the other kid...Who was it? Justin...something... Justin Moore. "Fuck, I don't want to do this." It had been dark out, stormy, the two boys had just maimed each other, and the council had kept everyone back, kept everyone out of it. Two kids. Barely eighteen. Too young for a fight like that, but Tarians didn't give a shit about ethics. They cared about dominance and prepping those two to run the Pride someday. They'd damn near killed each other. Grim was laying in the mud, eyes on his grandma, and Rose was losing her shit. Council members were holding her back as she screamed and clawed and fought to go to Grim…

Talon shoved the door open and stumbled out just so he could be out in the open and breathe again, but the memory wouldn't go away.

Ronin, young blond-haired best friend of Grim, practically raised by Rose, was hugging her tight as Grim died. Or at least they thought he was dying. They didn't know he was becoming the Reaper instead. The tears streaming down Rose's face as she watched her grandson bleeding out was something that had stayed with Talon for years. He'd worked hard to get rid of that memory, and Ronin had dug it back up.

He gripped the side of the pickup bed, locked his arms against it, and lifted his furious gaze to Ronin, who was leaning against the other side.

Ronin told him, "Rose just gave up a baby she was

helping raise to Vyr Daye and his mate, Riyah. Do you want to know why she gave that cub up?"

Part of him wanted to know every single thing about Rose, and part of him was terrified of seeing the deep parts of her. Why? Because those deep places would tether the man in him to her, but it would scare the lion off. Losing a mate had wrecked him. Now he was a monster who knew fear. Not in a fight, but on an emotional level. And scared animals either felt cornered and fought their way out...or they ran.

Louder, Ronin repeated, "Do you want to know why?"

"I would rather know why you are doing this," Talon snarled, feeling like Ronin was taking a knife down his torso and releasing his guts slowly.

Ronin's eyes were bright gold-green as he growled, "Partly, she gave him to the Red Dragon because it was best for the cub, and partly she did it for Vyr, who was losing his mind without offspring. But the biggest reason was that Rose was afraid to get attached to the cub, and have him taken away. So you see, she's given you a gift that you don't realize yet. She's given you her time, and she doesn't give that away lightly. Not unless she feels like the risk is worth it. Talon...she thinks your worth it, or you wouldn't have her attention at all." Ronin's eyes flashed with anger, and he lifted the side of his lip in a snarl. "Don't fuck it up."

The Alpha walked around the back of the truck and sauntered through the open gates of the lumber yard. He didn't look back. He'd just put a bomb in Talon's mind and was letting the time run out on it. Tick, tock, tick, tock.

He had fucked up. He shouldn't have ever pursued Rose. He wished he was different and worth it, like she thought he was, but the cold, hard truth was, he wasn't worth a damn to a woman like her. She deserved the world.

And what had he been doing since he'd come here?

He'd been staring out the windows, feeling trapped.

Looking at the road with a sense of urgency. A sense of longing.

He'd used sex with Rose as a coping mechanism to deal with the chaos of his life. He'd tried so hard to get his lion to anchor to this place and get him to stay.

To cut the chaos out of his life. He wanted his lion to let him keep her.

He'd failed. That much was evident by the bone-deep urge to run now. His lion was practically roaring for him to walk away from all of this.

Rose was a goddess and he was a fucking disaster.

Tick, tock, tick, tock.

And standing in this old, dusty parking lot, watching Ronin disappear behind a stack of lumber, he knew what he was going to do. What he had to do.

He couldn't keep a tender heart like Rose's safe. They weren't alike.

He'd tried so hard to fix his lion's roaming glitch that somewhere along the way he'd gone and fallen in love.

In love.

With a Pride member.

With a non-roamer.

A non-rogue.

With a steady woman who'd grown her roots deep and strong.

Fuck.

And the longer he stayed, the more he was going

to bond her to him and ruin her.

The longer he stayed, the more he was going to hurt Rose.

Tick, tock, tick, tock.

His heart was going to be very empty without her.

SEVEN

Rose had an idea.

A tiny inkling of the beginnings of an idea.

A little seed that could grow into something beautiful if she worked hard enough.

As she stood outside the florist, her attention drifting from the bouquets of roses sitting in the window to the woman inside, Annamora, talking to the manager about filling out an application for when they were hiring again, that little seed started to grow.

There was a flyer taped to the door, right under the building number, 1010. A loose corner of the paper was flapping in the wind, practically begging for Rose to pay attention to it. The flyer asked for flower growers to contact the shop so the owner could support other local small business as much as possible.

Inside, Annamora nodded and smiled as she said her goodbyes to the shop owner, but her smile had ghosts in it. The girls had all struck out on the job search today. Emerald was with Maris and Sora down the street, but Rose could see them from here. They were settling on a park bench, talking to each other. They looked upset.

They'd been sheltered and in an abusive situation in the Old Tarian Pride, made to feel like they were nothing. These women needed something to boost their confidence so they could start thriving in the New Tarian Pride. Because right now, they were still all scared as little bunnies and uncertain, heads lowered, eyes always on the ground. They had trouble talking to the males in the Pride, and they were good ones. All of them. Crass, sometimes rude, definitely perverted, but down to their core, they were good. And still, these lionesses were struggling to break free of their submissive habits.

But that flyer...

Something about it felt special.

She pulled out her phone and called Talon's number. It was her first time calling him, and butterflies beat their wings in her chest. She shifted her weight to the left, then to the right, fidgeting as the phone rang and rang. He was the first person she wanted to talk to about this. Honestly, he was the first person she wanted to tell anything to.

This is Talon, leave a message at the beep.

Beeeeeeeeeep.

Shoot. "Hi, it's me, Rose." She let off a nervous laugh and gripped the cell phone tighter. "I just had this idea. You know how I said I've been bored and having a hard time adjusting to retirement? What do you think about maybe me setting up the greenhouse as an income-earning flower-growing business? Oh, I can talk to you about this all later. See you so soon. Headed to dinner with the girls. I'm rambling. Talk soon."

She almost, almost said, "I love you." It was so close, the words right on the tip of her tongue, but instead she hung up quickly and exhaled a steadying breath. She'd called a man first. How very modern of her.

Tonight, she was going to buy the girls drinks and

cut loose, give them some time away from their own heads, because Talon had taught her something important. A break from the tough stuff, even if it was a small one, could make a world of difference for someone.

And tonight she would talk to Talon all about her greenhouse plans to get the girls back on their feet.

EIGHT

Angel Fire, New Mexico.

The other three envelopes tumbled right from Rose's fingertips to the ground, and she stared at the postcard.

It had been two weeks since Talon had disappeared without a word.

Two weeks since her world had gone dim and the colors had lost their vibrance.

Oh, he'd called her once a few days after he'd disappeared. She'd been in the greenhouse cleaning up and missed the call. The voicemail had been short and sweet. And heartbreaking.

His voice sounded gruff and thick. All he'd said was, "I'm so sorry, Wildcat." It had sounded like he was crying, but she knew better. Steel men like Talon Lawson didn't cry.

Emerald had kept her updated on where he was and how he was doing for the first week, but it had gotten too hard for Rose to know, so she'd asked Emerald not to talk about him anymore.

Her heart had no business breaking over a man she only spent a few days with. A man who had never made her any promises.

She tried to explain that to her heart, but the pitiful little thing refused to listen.

She'd forced herself to stop checking her phone for his messages and looking at the driveway expectantly, hoping his Chevelle would be rumbling toward her.

He owed her nothing, no explanation; he was free. There was no need for anger at him. He'd told her from the very beginning he would leave, and maybe the way he did it made it easier on both of them.

Honestly, she was grateful, because he'd reminded her that she wasn't done yet. That she was alive. That she was sexy, playful, and worth a damn. And that, in itself, was a great gift. And if that wasn't big enough, the deliveries started arriving a few days after he left. Over the last two weeks, everything she'd needed to fix up the house had arrived at her doorstep. Ronin and a couple of the boys from the Pride had started coming over and fixing the place up with her. On the deliveries, there was never a name to claim who paid for the supplies, but she knew it was him. Talon. Her Talon, even if he didn't know she thought of him that way.

Angel Fire, New Mexico.

Under the lettering, there was a picture of a beautiful mountain with ski slopes.

She turned the postcard over slowly and read the block print letters.

Hey Wildcat,

I swore I was going to make a clean break to make this easier on you. I've picked up and put down a dozen postcards in different places and talked myself out of sending them to you. I tried not to send you anything so you could forget about me, but the selfish side of me doesn't want you to forget. Apparently, I'm no good all around. All I think about is you.

I'm sorry.

Talon

Rose clutched the postcard to her chest and squeezed her eyes closed as a mixture of joy and regret washed through her. Her eyes burned with tears because she really *really* wished he was here, telling her those words instead of writing them from so far away.

Rose made her way to her fridge, lifted a magnet, and tacked the postcard under it. Then she pulled out her phone and texted him, knowing he would never text her back.

The snow looks beautiful in Angel Fire. I hope you find peace there. Send.

NINE

San Antonio, Texas

This one came on a Friday, one day shy of one week after the first one, and it had a package with it.

The postcard had a picture of a the Riverwalk, all lit up at night. It was beautiful. She flipped it over.

Wildcat,

It sure feels empty out on the road without you. I keep looking over at the passenger seat and imagining you sitting there, hand catching the wind out the open window, smile on your face, hair a beautiful mess. Emerald told me what you're trying to do for the girls. Giving them work in your greenhouse and teaching them a trade. Teaching them to plant. You're one helluva woman. Hopefully this little present helps. I wish I could do more. You deserve so much more.

I'm sorry.

Talon

After she put it on the fridge next to the last postcard, she opened the package and cried a little, hoping this would be the last postcard that brought tears.

It was a plastic container organized with flower seed packets, set in alphabetical order.

She hadn't gotten flowers from a man in decades. Well, that wasn't entirely true. Her grandson, Grim, sent her roses with the thorns cut off sometimes. Pink ones because they were her favorite. But that was her grandson, not a man courting her. Perhaps Talon didn't mean for it to feel big, but for her, this counted.

She texted him. This was the only time she allowed herself to—on postcard day. *Thank you for the flowers. They're beautiful and made me smile.* Send.

She pulled a red tack out of the drawer and pinned it to the city on the map she'd bought last week. She stuck it right into San Antonio, Texas.

And her silly little heart loved him still.

TEN

Oklahoma City, Oklahoma.

One week after the last post card.

This one had a black and white photo of the downtown.

Dear Wildcat,

I don't feel the same as I used to. I keep searching for something, but there's no joy in the looking anymore. Feels like I already found it and perhaps threw it away, not realizing what I had. I hope these are the right color. You deserve for a man to get things right.

I'm sorry.

Talon

The post card came with a delivery of a dozen rose bushes.

Her heart didn't hurt so much on this one. Perhaps it was his note that gave her hope.

Ronin had stopped working on the porch when she'd come in with the mail. He'd stuck his head in the door and watched her ritual.

Read the postcard.

Put it on the fridge.

Stick the tack in the map so she didn't feel so far away from him.

This time the ritual was different, though. She didn't cry.

Ronin asked, "Are the pink rose bushes from him?"

Rose nodded.

Ronin's smile was sad, but still, Rose didn't cry. After he patted the doorframe twice and went back to work, Rose pulled out her cell phone to finish her tradition.

You got the color right. Send.

ELEVEN

Topeka, Kansas

Three days after the last.

The picture was big, beautiful sunflowers.

Hey Wildcat,

Been sick. I think it's my lion. Nothing serious. I think I just maybe broke my own heart.

I'm so sorry for what I've done to us. I feel like I should lead with that on every postcard I send. You don't have to forgive me. I sure as hell don't. I ask Emerald about you. I don't know what I'm doing.

I'm sorry.

Talon

This one worried her.

Sounds like you have a silly heart, too. Sometimes, they want what they want, and who are we to convince them they're wrong? I'm still here. Send.

Her heart hurt as she stuck the post card on the fridge and the tack in the map. She didn't understand his need to wander.

But her heart loved him still.

TWELVE

Dodge City, Kansas

Two days after the last.

The postcards were coming faster now.

Hey Wildcat,

I have an admission. I look for postcards everywhere because I know when you get one from me, you'll text me. It's becoming a little addiction. I hang onto every word of your post-postcard text. I've read them a hundred times. Pull them up at truck stops when I'm getting gas, stare at them when I'm laying in hotel beds. You did something to me. To my animal. I can't tell if it's good or bad yet, but I can say one thing. The three days I spent with you were the best days I can remember. Thank you for making me feel alive again.

I'm sorry.

Talon

She held this one for a while before she put it on the fridge with the others. Read it over and over like he did with her texts.

And then she did her tradition. Post card up on the fridge in line with the others, a pin in the map.

This time, she wanted to give him something to really think about.

I wish you would come home. Send.

And her little heart loved him more and more.

THIRTEEN

Telluride, Colorado

Rose read those two words over and over. The picture was historic downtown with the mountain she lived on towering in the background.

Telluride, Colorado.

Could it be? Rose turned the card over.

Wildcat,

Go put the tack in the map. Have you figured out what I've been drawing for you yet?

Shocked, Rose looked up at the map she'd hung on her wall by the fridge. She put a red tack in Telluride and completed the outline of a heart.

Tears burned her eyes as she continued reading...

I should've told you how I really felt about you before I left, but I needed to work on some stuff. I spent the first few weeks beating myself up for not being enough, for not being steady, for not being able to just stay put for you. And then I got mad enough to start working my way back to you, and fuck what my lion asked for. Eventually, the old rogue grew a heart in the old empty chest cavity of his and wanted to go back to you too, because I figured out something big over these last weeks. I'm nothing without you. Been sick without you. Been empty without you. I'm sorry I had to do this to us. Sorry I had to draw you a heart on a map instead of just telling you...I love you, Rose.

Talon

Telluride, Colorado

Chest heaving with her breath, Rose dropped the postcard and ran to the door. She threw it open and staggered out onto the new porch.

Across the clearing, he was there, her Talon.

Behind him, the towering pines swayed this way and that in the breeze, but Talon didn't move. The way he looked at her made her feel beautiful.

"Talon," she uttered brokenly. She bolted down the stairs, ran across the snow right for him.

He was crying, her steel man. His dark eyes were rimmed with tears, and he jogged for her, and then ran, and then his arms were out to catch her.

Okay.

Okay, Rose.

Go ahead and fall the rest of the way.

He's catching you.

Talon lifted her off the ground and hugged her tight, his beard soft against her cheeks as she nuzzled him on one side and then the other. Her lioness was purring so loud, but she didn't care. Not anymore. He could see all of her, and it was all right. He was the only one who could see all of her.

"Swear it," she said in a ragged whisper.

He would understand because he *knew* her. He had since she'd healed him. He really saw her, really understood her.

"I swear I won't run again, Rose. I won't go anywhere without you by my side."

There was an unbreakable oath in his tone. A promise in the purring that rattled his throat and matched her own. Their lions were talking. He wouldn't do this to them again. He'd tortured his nomadic animal with an aching heart, and now he wouldn't run anymore. Not from her, because she belonged to him, and he belonged to her.

Some men required patience.

They needed complete freedom to figure out love was never a cage in the first place.

That love had been the freedom all along.

Talon settled her on her feet and cupped her cheeks, wiped her tears with his thumbs, and searched her eyes. "Forgive me."

"Silly man," she murmured, "you made me no promises. You were already forgiven before you even left. I just missed you."

"You told me to come home." He scanned the clearing and the house, and then his dark eyes landed back on her. "You have to know...I didn't understand what home was until I met you."

And if he hadn't drawn her the heart with his travels or said he loved her on the postcard, well...she would've known his feelings from that admission. Love was finding a home in someone.

Rose's smile stretched her whole face, and she

melted into him, hugged him so tight and rested her cheek against his chest, right over his drumming heart. Her lioness had picked him. *She* had picked him, and now he'd chosen her back. All these years, she'd thought she was destined to be alone. To watch the couples pair up around her because she'd already had her time. She'd had her chance when she was young. She'd thought those three most important words would never belong to her again.

But Fate hadn't been done with her yet. It hadn't been done with Talon either.

"Hey Talon?" she whispered.

"Mmm?" he asked, smiling down at her knowingly.

"I love you, too."

Want more of these characters?

The New Tarian Pride series is a standalone series set in the Damon's Mountains Universe.
More of these characters can be found in the following series:

Saw Bears

Gray Back Bears

Fire Bears

Boarlander Bears

Harper's Mountains

Kane's Mountains

Red Havoc Panthers

Sons of Beasts

Daughters of Beasts

About the Author

T.S. Joyce is devoted to bringing hot shifter romances to readers. Hungry alpha males are her calling card, and the wilder the men, the more she'll make them pour their hearts out. She werebear swears there'll be no swooning heroines in her books. It takes tough-as-nails women to handle her shifters.

She lives in a tiny town, outside of a tiny city, and devotes her life to writing big stories. Foodie, wolf whisperer, ninja, thief of tiny bottles of awesome smelling hotel shampoo, nap connoisseur, movie fanatic, and zombie slayer, and most of this bio is true.

Bear Shifters? Check

Smoldering Alpha Hotness? Double Check

Sexy Scenes? Fasten up your girdles, ladies and gents, it's gonna to be a wild ride.

For more information on T. S. Joyce's work,
visit her website at
www.tsjoyce.com

Made in the USA
Monee, IL
03 July 2023